The Godmother

PATRICIA FISHER MYSTERY ADVENTURES BOOK 8

STEVE HIGGS

D1520173

This book is dedicated to Alison Jones who gave Patricia Rose Fisher a maiden name at last. Thank you, Alison, for your excellent suggestion.

Contents

Robbery Versus Theft

Alistair and I enjoyed dinner in Shinsen Sushi, a plush Japanese restaurant on the eighteenth deck. It opened in the period between my stays onboard the Aurelia, replacing a Mexican restaurant so tonight was my first visit. Alistair was off duty and dressed in a jacket and tie for once instead of his captain's white uniform. I loved the way he looked in his uniform, but this was good too.

The sushi was freshly prepared by a chef at a horseshoe shaped table that surrounded him. It was completely different from the intimate, just the two of us, experience we usually enjoyed as the table seated twelve. Different turned out to be fun though, conversation ranging from one topic to the next as the people seated around us brought lots of new things to discuss.

After dinner, we took a walk around the ship, strolling arm in arm like a couple in love for that is what we are. Accepting that I was in love with Alistair created a new problem which I was yet to overcome or even put much thought to – I live in England, and he lives on a ship which perpetually navigates the globe. We were both skirting the subject for the time being because there was a greater problem yet to overcome.

It was during our stroll, as we approached the stairwell to take us up to the top deck and my suite that we happened upon what was clearly an incident of some kind. I felt Alistair's body tense as he saw two of his security detail talking to a distressed couple.

I took my arm from his, saying, 'Go.'

He hurried forward, jogging to get there which brought attention his way. Seeing who it was, the guards snapped out crisp salutes. The nearer of the two addressed him, 'Good evening, sir.'

'Good evening,' he replied, focussing his attention on the couple after a brief nod to his crewmen. 'How can I be of service?' he asked the passengers.

'There was a robbery, sir,' announced the guard who was yet to speak. 'We discovered Mr and Mrs Bisset moments after the event. They both seem quite ... confused,' the man explained, searching for the right word. I judged it might not be the word he would have used if the couple were not standing next to him.

'Very good, Lieutenant Zaki. Let's get them back to their cabin and deal with it there.' As always, Alistair took control. It was his gift, and the reason he was captain of an enormous vessel with thousands of crew and passengers under his protection.

Mr and Mrs Bisset were probably from France I guessed when Alistair launched into fluent French. My French is terrible to say the least, so I could tell that was what they were speaking, but didn't even try to keep up with what was being said. I tagged along behind the party though, expecting that this would prove to be no more than a brief hiatus to our plans.

What the lieutenants said about the couple seeming confused was instantly obvious as they didn't seem to know where their cabin was.

'This is how we found them, sir,' explained Lieutenant Zaki. 'They hadn't called for help but were clearly distressed when we chanced upon them. The only piece of information they are both sure of is that they have been robbed.'

'That would suggest the thief was aggressive and threatening,' I pointed out, being a little pedantic but also trying to establish if the thief had been armed, and if so, what with?

With a thoughtful glance in my direction, Alistair addressed the Bissets again, asking them for more detail about the robbery, I guessed. They didn't have answers to those questions either.

Alistair kept his attention on the passengers when he handed out his instructions. 'Hamond, get their accommodation assignment from central registry and have Dr Davis meet me there, please.'

'They are staying in a cabin on deck twelve, sir,' advised Hamond about two seconds later, proving he already had the presence of mind to find their cabin for himself. We were going to deck twelve it seemed, the two lieutenants doing their best to guide the addled couple in the right direction.

Alistair dropped back a few feet to speak with me. 'Do you want to go back to your suite? I'll try not to take too long.'

'I think I'll tag along if that's okay. You make me feel safe,' I was toying with him, of course, since I had an armed bodyguard shadowing me no more than five yards away. Agent Garrett of Scotland Yard was with me for my protection because of the bigger issue I mentioned earlier. As part of our date night, there was an agreed clause where neither of us was allowed to bring up the subject of the shadow hanging over me, so I did my part and pushed the uninvited thoughts back out of my head lest they make it to my tongue.

Alistair smiled at me teasing him anyway. 'I thought you might. Did you know this isn't the first incident like this?'

I did not. 'How many have there been?'

'Two previous to this one, if this turns out to be the same thing. The passengers in the previous incidents had each lost several hours of their evening and had been robbed. You're right about the robbery versus theft thing though because there was no suggestion of violence. In both the previous cases, the thefts were conducted without violence. It's strange,' he said, searching for the right word. 'The passengers handed over their valuables – money and jewellery mostly – as if unable to resist doing so but had no clear memory of the event or of their thief.'

I thought about the case, wondering what the victims might have in common. Their confused state was puzzling. Why didn't they remember the thief?

It would not help the captain that some of his best people were seconded to me in secret because of the bigger problem we were not talking about tonight. At the Bissets' cabin, Hamond used his universal card to open the door before helping them inside. Commander Ochi, the deputy captain, and head of ship security, arrived moments later.

At that point, I was pleased to hear Alistair pass the incident over to his deputy as I wasn't sure how involved he would get. As captain, he acted as if everyone on board were his personal guest and took great interest in everything that happened to them, most especially when it was a negative experience. However, with Commander Ochi in attendance, there was no reason for him to remain behind. He made his excuses, and behind me Agent Wayne Garrett opened the Bissets' cabin door to let us out.

Showing me that he was in a playful mood, and catching me completely by surprise, Alistair pinched my bum as I went out the door. I squeaked in surprise, making Agent Garrett spin around to check on me as my cheeks coloured.

Alistair, earning himself a punishment I was yet to devise, played the innocent, giving me a genuine expression when he asked, 'Is everything all right, dear?'

Team HQ

S ome time later, lying in bed with Alistair kissing my shoulder, the inevitable subject of the bigger problem arose. 'Have the team made any progress?' he asked.

Teasing him again, I replied, 'I thought that subject was a non-topic.'

'It is now well after midnight, Patricia. It was nice to be able to ignore it for a few hours, but the Godmother is here, and I will quite happily 'accidentally' shove her overboard if it removes the danger to you.'

Alistair's question prompted me to slip out of the bed. Finding my clothes, I said, 'Agent Garrett will be asleep now. I should check in with the team.' I think Alistair wanted to argue, but he didn't, sliding from my bed and into his clothes so he could accompany me. We moved silently, taking my two sleeping dachshunds with me. If I left them behind, they might elect to go back to sleep and remain in their bed in my bedroom, but I wouldn't be able to guarantee they wouldn't howl at my absence or go looking for me and it remained imperative that Agent Garrett not know about my night time excursions.

Twelve decks down and almost at the bottom of the passenger part of the ship, we arrived at team HQ.

It was quiet inside and lit by a single lamp above a computer desk loaded with additional equipment not normally found in a deck eight cabin. The man sitting in front of the computer desk, turned his body to face us.

'Good evening, madam,' he nodded his head dutifully first at me and then Alistair. 'Captain.'

I went over to the desk and pulled him into a gentle hug, being careful not to touch his left arm and shoulder where he suffered a bullet wound a few days ago. 'Hello, Jermaine. Anything to report?'

Jermaine shook his head. 'No. I think she is simply too savvy for us to catch her out like this.' He pushed his chair back from the monitor screen and stood up, stretching his long body to work out the kinks from being scrunched up for so long.

We were crammed into cabin 34782 on deck eight which I booked for a detective friend of mine to stay in. Who am I? Good question. I used to be Mrs Charlie Fisher, bored housewife with a rubbish job as a cleaner. I probably would have remained in that job and that life forever had I not caught Charlie quite literally with his pants down in my best friend's bedroom.

Our divorce is right around the corner, but I have a more pressing matter to deal with first, that of the Godmother. The Godmother sits at the head of an organised crime syndicate and she wants me dead. That's problem enough, but it gets worse because she is so powerful and well connected that she cannot be caught by the authorities. Her organisation had been around long enough to have corrupt people inside every law enforcement agency on the planet, plus politicians in their pockets, judges, lawyers ... you get the picture.

She can't buy everyone, of course, but since I don't know who might be on her payroll, trusting anyone is decidedly dodgy. That leaves me and my friends in a precarious position and forced to try to work out a way to defeat her using just our own wit and resources.

If I know who she is, why can't I just have her arrested? Good question. The answer is even better. She is on board posing as a middle-aged woman from the west of England. Supposedly on the holiday of a lifetime with her long-suffering husband, in order to do anything, I need proof. So far, what I can prove, is that she is a middle-aged woman from the west of England on the holiday of a lifetime with her long-suffering husband. She came on board the Aurelia using her real name, and she really is from the west of England. It would also appear that she is actually married to the man she is here with.

It was possible to find a few cracks in her story, enough for me to be sure I had the right person. It was small things, like not having a job. Neither one of them has an employment record, which isn't exactly a big warning sign, but it's a start. The dog she keeps with her, isn't hers. My assumption is that she went out and got herself a dachshund before coming on board just so she could show common ground between the two of us: she's here for me, after all.

Mike Atwell, my detective sergeant friend from home, had to dig deep to prove her school records were forged. Verity Tuppence, formerly Verity Arkwright, did not attend Yate Grammar School for Girls as her records show. She was educated at Fulmington Private School for Girls and then attended Oxford where she achieved a double first in law and politics. I had to look Fulmington school up because I had never heard of it and discovered it to be considered one of the three top schools in England.

Daddy had money. Daddy also had a fake life, hiding what I assumed to be a criminal empire his daughter then inherited. There was enough misdirection and lying to convince me I was being hunted by one of the most dangerous women on the planet but knowing and being able to do something about it were two different things.

If she wants me dead, why is she meeting me for lunches and pretending to be my friend? Another great question, and one I can only guess at an answer to. She has been on board and in my company for more than two weeks. Like my party of friends, she came aboard in Canada, finding herself involved in the terrible events involving former deputy captain Robert Schooner. If all she wanted was my body in the morgue, she could have just let Schooner kill me. He certainly had the chance, but she chose to shoot him with a spearfishing gun, saving me in the process. I believe she did that because she wants me to die in a way that she can control.

Three days ago, Jermaine was shot. The wound is healing though I see him taking painkillers to numb the discomfort he still feels, and his left arm is in a sling. Verity arranged to have him shot, that I am almost certain of. A high-powered rifle was used, and such a thing ought to be impossible to smuggle onboard. Ought to be, but not for a master criminal and organised crime overlord.

The working theory was that she had many trusted lieutenants on board, each was most likely a trained and deadly killer. Worse yet was the probability that she had bought members of the security team. Robert Schooner had done much the same, leveraging old relationships and secrets he could expose to get himself back on board. Verity would just buy the people or have their families threatened to coerce them if they failed to comply.

What terrified me most about it all was the likelihood that Verity planned to hurt more of my friends. If shooting Jermaine was a deliberate act to weaken me, was she planning to eliminate more of them until she felt I was broken and alone? Was her aim to reduce me to a lonely, friendless mess and then, when I had no one left to turn to, kill me herself?

Like I said, it was a terrifying thought, but one I had to entertain. She didn't know Jermaine was alive, the bullet narrowly missed his heart, and we faked his death when it occurred to me that he might have been the true target that day. Molly, my housemaid left the ship in Iceland mere moments before it sailed. A call from Alistair set up her entry into the Purple Star academy in California. If she passed their entry tests, she would be trained as one of the security team. It was an exciting development for her, and one which I heavily endorsed because it got her out of harm's way. Unfortunately, if I was correct about Verity's intentions, she had plenty of targets left.

So here we were, trying to work out how to expose her. We needed evidence of her activities that we could use, and a law enforcement agency prepared to take her on. So far, I had neither. The screen Jermaine had been watching, showed the inside of her cabin. In line with her fake personality, she and her husband were staying in one of the small cabins way down in the bowels of the ship. Getting cameras inside it was easy enough, friends on the security team, ones I felt sure I could trust, had placed them there when Verity went to breakfast a few days ago.

Unfortunately, they were failing to yield anything of use.

The ship would arrive in Scotland during the night, docking in Glasgow, a vibrant city on the west coast. It was to be a thirty-six-hour stopover, with a quick hop from there to Dublin in Ireland the next night. Verity was due to depart the ship in Southampton, which was both good and bad. Good because it meant whatever devious and despicable plan she was working had to be played out in less than a week. It was bad for the exact same reason.

Sailing from Reykjavik in Iceland three days ago, I chose to make a few phone calls. Given how many troops the Godmother potentially had on board, I felt it was time to add some secret passengers of my own. She didn't know about Mike Atwell, a detective sergeant friend from home in whose cabin we now stood, and she thought Jermaine was dead. The longer they remained a secret the better, but it wasn't enough, so I called in the A team. In Glasgow, some old friends were joining us, and I couldn't wait to see them.

Noise coming from the cabin's solitary bedroom turned into Mike Atwell a few seconds later, the ageing police detective staggering through the door and into the living area with a yawn splitting his face. When it subsided, he went into a routine of scratching himself.

'What time is it?' he asked.

Jermaine replied, 'Almost three.'

Mike nodded as he fought another yawn. 'Almost my turn then.' The chaps were working in shifts, watching Verity the Godmother either in her cabin, or elsewhere around the ship as she moved about among the passengers. So far they had identified sixteen possible employees/henchmen – people, mostly men, who she had met with. Now, the trusted members of the ship's security team, four lieutenants who I knew well enough to believe were on my side, were tailing the men, and digging into their pasts. They might all be in the Godmother's employment, or it could be none of them and we needed to know which it was.

'I think we should abandon the surveillance,' I stated. When the three men looked my way, I clarified, 'On the cabin cameras, I mean. It was a long shot that she might hold meetings in her room and discuss something incriminating.'

Sadly, no one argued. We had limited resources and could not afford to waste them on a venture which looked unlikely to yield a result.

Jermaine asked, 'So what do we try next?'

Secrets and Lies

A t breakfast in my suite, Barbie leaned in to hiss the same question, 'So what do we do next, Patty?' She was speaking quietly to avoid Agent Garrett hearing her. He was dressed for the day in his usual copper's outfit of cheap suit, shirt, and tie with sensible boots on his feet. The suit jacket needed to fit badly to hide the weapon hidden under his left arm.

He was seated in the central living area and probably wasn't paying any attention to what we were saying anyway. He had the television on and a newspaper from England on his lap. A cup of tea steamed on a side table by his elbow.

I checked his way, convinced myself he couldn't hear us, but dropped my voice anyway. 'Get closer,' I answered her. 'I've met her for a couple of lunches and such but have been keeping her at arm's length since Reykjavik. Ever since I worked out who she is. I need to change that now and be with her as much as I can. Jermaine, Mike, and some of the others will be watching and tailing anyone that gets near to her. Deepa and Anders are on her husband, Walter,' I told her, talking about Lieutenants Deepa Bhukari and Anders Pippin, two of the four members of the security team working with me. 'There has to be a way to crack her.'

'We need to get inside her organisation's administration,' Barbie whispered.

'I know,' I replied, glumly. It had been one of our earliest considerations that the way to catch her was to find a way inside her operation. Barbie had poured countless hours into it back in the UK not long after I received the first threat. The Godmother's dealings were conducted inside the dark web, a hidden portion of the internet only accessible with the correct passcodes. All Barbie found was a couple of documents that referenced the organisation. She had tried again in the last few days, spending money to obtain sophisticated dark web software that would enable her to scour the darkest areas of the internet. However, her searches had all proved fruitless, and would continue to do so until such time as we obtained a passcode to the intranet portal for her organisation.

It was the golden ticket, the winning shot, but how were we to obtain such a thing?

'That's your plan?' Barbie sounded deeply worried. 'Get closer to the woman who wants you dead. What then?'

I had a few plans up my sleeve I was yet to share with Barbie and a big surprise in store for her in Glasgow. I was getting better at being devious, though I used my dark plans for good, not evil. I had to be close to Verity because there was something I had noticed; it was my primary reason for spending more time with her. If I was right, we would need to change our plans, but I wouldn't know without getting a good deal closer.

'There remains the option of having Alistair shove her overboard,' I replied deadpan.

Barbie's jaw dropped. 'Patty, you wouldn't!' she hissed.

I shook my head. 'No, I wouldn't.' I couldn't come down to the Godmother's level. It was a limitation that stacked the deck in the crime gang's favour. Verity and her minions could maim and kill, but my side couldn't, no matter how just it might feel.

'What about Wayne?' Barbie asked. 'Don't you think you should bring him into the fold? He'd be better able to protect you if he knew what you suspected.'

She was right and I knew it, but my argument hadn't changed since the start of this. Agent Garrett was trustworthy, that was what we all believed. He'd thrown himself in the way of a bullet to save my life and you don't get much more committed than that. It wasn't Wayne I didn't trust, it was anyone else in his organisation he might report to. If I told him Verity Tuppence was the Godmother and she was on board, could I then trust him to not tell anyone else? Despite the public mission to be my bodyguard, I believed the real reason for his presence close to me was to watch for the Godmother and be able to report back up his chain. The team in Scotland Yard wanted to catch her but I refused to believe they were not compromised.

I shook my head. 'I can't.'

We ate the rest of our breakfast in silence, Barbie chomping her way through a piece of seared tuna with brown rice and courgette on the side. It was hardly breakfast fayre, the gym bunny showing off why she has zero cellulite yet again. I had eggs Benedict with lashings of Hollandaise sauce, demonstrating why my bottom did not, and never had, looked anything like hers.

To switch the subject, I told her about the French couple the previous evening.

'Oh, I heard about that from Deepa,' Barbie revealed. 'It's the third incident like it,' Barbie pointed out.

'Yes, I heard that from Alistair. Don't worry though, I'm not going to poke my nose into it.'

'That doesn't sound like you,' Barbie commented. 'I think the captain put two guys on it yesterday, making it their exclusive task to track down the culprit.'

'Who did he choose?' I asked her.

'Two guys I don't know,' she admitted. 'They joined the crew when I was in England. I think their names are Zaki and Hamond. Zaki is Egyptian, that's about all I know,' she told me with a shrug.

It was the two men I met last night in the passageway with the victims.

Just then, a knock at the door caught my attention. It also woke both my dachshunds, who flew from the couch, barking as they sprinted across the carpet to repel the invaders. Muscle memory made me wait for my butler to answer the door, a full two seconds passing before I remembered he wasn't here and went myself. Alistair had offered to give me a replacement, but I declined, not wanting someone else to fill Jermaine's shoes, if only for a short time.

I got only two paces, before a polite cough stopped me. 'If you please, Mrs Fisher.' Wayne was just doing his job, being super-cautious because there could be a gunman on the other side of the door waiting to shoot me when it opened.

I watched him approach the door, his gun drawn. With extreme caution, he paused not in front of the door, but along the wall from it. 'Who is it?' he demanded loudly.

'It's Baker and Schneider, Supercop. Open the door.' Lieutenants Baker and Schneider were two of the Aurelia's security team who I knew quite well. They had saved my life more than once and were part of my secret team alongside Bhukari and Pippin.

The two men came into the suite, doffing their hats and offering them to Agent Garret for him to hang up. They got a hand gesture in response, all three chuckling at the banter.

Barbie waved. 'Hi, guys. What's happening?'

'Nothing much,' Schneider replied. 'The ship, apart from the strange robbery case, is quiet. It will get busy again tonight as we dock in Scotland and need to manage all the passengers getting on and off, but for now there isn't much happening.'

That might be true for their colleagues, but both Baker and Schneider were on overwatch duty for me, carrying out surveillance much like Mike and Jermaine. They couldn't say that in front of Agent Garrett for precisely the reasons I have just explained.

'Strange robbery case?' echoed Wayne. He didn't approve of my general sleuthing while on board. In his opinion, it exposed me to unnecessary risk, and it wasn't as if I were being paid for it. I help the security team out because it gives me pleasure to do so, and because I have a plan up my sleeve none of them were privy to yet. It was going to remain that way until such time as I could be sure it was what I wanted and could actually achieve it.

I let Lieutenant Baker explain the strange robberies to Agent Garrett and make it look like that was why Baker and Schneider had come to my suite, there being no other obvious reason for their visit. That was until they got to the ruse they'd come prepared with.

'It's about Jermaine, Mrs Fisher,' Baker announced in sombre tones.

I let my smile fall, acting out the part of a person still grieving their friend. I didn't like deceiving Agent Garrett like this, but until I could be certain it wasn't necessary, I had to keep him in the dark.

'His body will be repatriated to Jamaica from Scotland when we dock there. The captain plans to hold a small ceremony in the chapel on deck eighteen at four o'clock tomorrow.'

I nodded my head, making it look like I was having trouble finding words. After a moment to gather myself, I said, 'Very good. Thank you for letting me know.'

Barbie let a solitary tear fall and came in close so we could hold hands – it felt like what we might do if this were real.

Agent Garrett chose to use the moment against me. 'Can I assume, Mrs Fisher, that given what happened to Jermaine, you will not be pursuing this latest robbery case?'

His question, or should that be assumption, irritated me. So much so that I almost snapped that I would be investigating it, but I wrestled my tongue under control. 'No, Agent Garrett, I will not be pursuing the case. The Aurelia's team can figure this one out for themselves.'

Baker and Schneider chose to make good their escape; they had tasks to perform after all. Breakfast was complete, Barbie was going to the gym, and I was taking the dachshunds for a walk where I planned to bump into Verity. Finding her by accident would be easy enough because I had no less than three people watching her.

The Godmother

It was still too cold on the deck of the ship to be walking the dogs outside. We were sailing south from Iceland to Scotland but not by enough to make a worthwhile change in the temperature. It would be a couple of weeks – once the ship left Southampton bound for the Caribbean - before the air would get back to something one might call balmy and pleasant.

To that end, I was walking the girls around inside the ship. They have been trained to use a rather clever, and expensive, indoor doggy toilet so the walks were almost always just for exercise. Mike was good enough to let me know Verity was in the mall on the sixteenth deck where she was having breakfast. His communication came via text message which I immediately deleted to be sure Agent Garrett couldn't see it. He shadowed me closely as always, walking near but not next to me unless I ever invited him to. When I spotted her - my timing impeccable and planned - she was just leaving, little Rufus her dachshund, tugging at his lead as he scrambled to follow his nose.

'Verity!' I called, waving my right hand in the air to get her attention. By her side was her husband, Walter. A tall, thin man standing roughly six and a half feet tall, he hardly ever spoke. In fact, Jermaine and Mike, who had been watching the couple in their cabin for days, reported that he never spoke there either.

He spent most of his time watching the television or reading. With Verity, the couple were out and about doing things most days, taking advantage of the shows, restaurants, cinemas, and other entertainments during the day. Of an evening, Verity would drink a small sherry from a supply she had and make entries in her journal. According to Mike and Jermaine, she rarely spoke to Walter either. It was an odd relationship, but perhaps one that is normal for a crazy crime boss worth billions and ready to kill at a moment's notice.

I closed the distance, making sure she had seen me and calling to Rufus so his attention would be drawn to my dogs, Anna and Georgie. Of course, Rufus wasn't his real name, though Verity hadn't thought to check his collar tag and I didn't bother to point it out - what would that achieve? It was another item to note from our surveillance that once inside their cabin, poor Rufus got completely ignored, as one might expect with a dog whose sole purpose was to be a prop. Thankfully, neither of them were mean to the little dog, just neglectful.

Rufus tried to run to see Anna and Georgie, his little claws skittering on the marble tile floor. Verity waved back. She had no choice, not if she wanted to maintain the façade of being my friend.

'Hi, Patricia. How are you?' she asked cautiously. She was with me when the news of Jermaine's fake death was broken because I had planned it to happen that way and we hadn't spoken properly since. I hadn't felt any need to spend time in her company and had a perfect excuse in my grief.

I made sure my face bore a suitably sad expression when I replied. 'I'm bearing up. The shock of it has passed, but ... is it okay if we don't talk about it?'

She reached out with her left hand to touch my arm in comfort. 'Of course, Patricia. Whatever you need. I'm here if you do want to talk. Goodness knows I don't get much conversation out of Walter.' Walter, standing not five feet away, didn't bother to express any emotion at her complaint.

'Actually,' I turned and started walking in the direction I expected her to go – back toward her cabin – I was hoping you might be free to spend some time together today. I could use some company who isn't ... affected by it, I suppose is what I am trying to say. I love Barbie to bits, but she is wallowing in her grief so terribly.'

'Will your hunky bodyguard be accompanying us?' she asked, eyeing Wayne up lasciviously. 'Perhaps we should go to one of the pools. I rather think I would like to see him in a swimsuit.'

I almost asked her if she was serious but decided instead to jump at the chance. If we went to a pool, and some of the same people Mike had seen near her in the last few days showed up there in their shorts or bikinis, then it would be just too much for coincidence.

'What a great idea!' I beamed. 'Oh, Verity, that sounds marvellous! Let's get our things right away.' I was laying the enthusiasm on thick, giving her no chance to back out if it had been a joke. Pausing to speak with Walter as he trailed along wordlessly in our wake, I said, 'That's okay, isn't it, Walter? Can you manage without your wife for a few hours? I'd like to borrow her.'

It didn't look as though he was going to respond for a beat, but then I got a barely perceptible shrug, and one of the first words I'd ever heard him say. 'S'pose.' I took that to be as close to a yes as I was going to get.

Seizing it anyway, I shot a sad smile at Agent Garrett. 'Will you accompany me to the pool on deck eighteen, Wayne?'

His eyebrows were more articulate than Walter's entire face. They said, you haven't given me any choice, Mrs Fisher, and though I would dearly love to argue, I will at least be able to see if anyone has a weapon there even though I won't be able to carry mine and will need to keep it in a bag. Like I said; articulate eyebrows. His lips said, 'Very good, Mrs Fisher.'

'Do you know they serve morning cocktails there?' I asked Verity, making sure I didn't gush with excitement, but also thinking that it might not be a bad idea for me to have a go at getting her a little merry. Who knows what might slip out if I got her well-oiled?

We agreed to meet near the pool area in half an hour. That gave us both enough time to shave our legs and pack an appropriate pool bag of items. My legs didn't need shaving, of course, rekindling my relationship with Alistair had ensured such things were already attended to. I did, however, need time to get my chess pieces into position. No sooner was Wayne in his room to change and pack a bag, than I was on the phone.

'You're going to do what?' Mike asked once I was done explaining.

'Get her drunk,' I repeated. 'It can't be that hard. It's not like I need her hardcore whammed off her face, just lubricated enough to start talking. I need you to meet Baker and Bhukari at the deck eighteen security post as soon as you can get there. They will fit you up with a uniform.'

'Hold on,' Mike interrupted. 'What uniform? Did I just miss a big part of your latest mad plan, or did you conveniently skip something? The plan was for me to remain out of sight.'

'You're just going to be one of the barmen, Mike. I called Lieutenant Baker before I called you. All you need to do is make sure that when I come to get drinks, you don't put any alcohol in mine and put an extra shot in hers. Trust me when I tell you that putting on a crew uniform makes you invisible.'

'Aren't I a little old to be a member of the crew?' he persisted, not entirely sold on my latest idea.

I shook my head even though he couldn't see it at the other end of the phone. 'Not at all, Mike. There are plenty of crew in their sixties.'

'I'm still in my fifties,' he protested, sounding hurt.

'Yeah, that's what I'm saying,' I tried to bluff my way past my error, thinking he looked like he was in his sixties, 'they have lots who are far older than you.' I put lots of emphasis on the 'far' part of that sentence.

Mike wasn't buying it. 'Yeah, whatever, Patricia. Okay, so I'm the barman for the next couple of hours. You want me to fiddle the drinks and see if I can recognise any of the people at the pool as people I have seen speaking with her or that undertaker-looking character she is married to.'

His comment made me giggle, though there was little funny about our situation. Walter would have made a perfect undertaker. Or perhaps a mortician though if he ever fell asleep on the job, they might accidentally embalm him.

'I'll see you there,' I promised, thanking him at the same time.

'Hey, Patricia,' he caught me just as I was about to hang up.

'Yes, Mike?'

'Wear something sexy.' The phone went dead as he started to laugh at the other end.

I frowned at my reflection. 'Cheeky git.' I would wear my standard one piece, the same as I always did. Barbie might get away with going to the pool wearing a shoelace and little else, but I fitted squarely into the demographic of normal which meant my tummy got covered up in public.

Operation Drunk as a Skunk

The more I thought about it, the more sense it made to get Verity absolutely bat-faced. I thought of the times I'd had one too many and the torrent of rubbish that would dribble from my lips. Not that I had done that in a couple of decades, but the memory of such things lingers. I needed her drunk enough to gabble without thought, but not so drunk that she failed to make sense. I certainly had to judge it carefully, because I didn't want her to become suspicious of the leading questions I planned to ask her, or to remember them afterwards.

Walking down to deck eighteen, with the dogs safely tucked away in my suite and Wayne as always on my shoulder, I did my best to quell the rising butterflies. Why hadn't this occurred to me before? I might catch her out and have this whole thing sewn up before we got to Scotland. All I needed was a way to expose her secrets. I wasn't going to be able to topple her empire, so what I needed was enough incriminating evidence against her to force her to back off. Or, better yet, undeniable proof that would see her and others locked up. Could I pull this off?

I turned a corner, leaving a passageway and strolling into the open-plan deck area with the pool. It might be cold outside, but the pool was popular, filled with passengers enjoying the amenities and warm temperature at which they ensured the water and poolside was maintained. Verity spotted me and waved, then cut her eyes at Wayne. Wearing a loose top unzipped to show off his pecs, and a pair of cotton shorts which let the world see his muscular thighs, he was what a younger woman might call eye-candy. I suspected Verity would say the same if her smile was anything to go by.

'I picked us some good seats already,' Verity bragged once I was close enough. 'I got two together,' she told Wayne. 'I figured you would want to position yourself a distance away so you can do your moody, macho, staring-at-everyone-silently thing.'

Wayne gave her a mirthless smile and walked away, looking for a spot from where he could watch me just as Verity predicted. As he moved away, Verity mouthed taking a bite out of his bottom. 'And you have him staying in your suite with you all the time, Patricia. I don't know how you do it.' She nudged my arm as she showed me the two loungers and indicated I should pick one. 'Tell me,' she begged, a cheeky expression on her face. 'Have you accidentally on purpose seen him naked yet? Does he have a big ...'

'Can I get you some drinks, ladies,' a familiar voice interrupted her just in the nick of time.

I turned my head, craning it slightly to look behind me at Mike bedecked in steward's livery. 'Yes, please,' I replied. 'How about a couple of gin and tonics?' I suggested.

'Goodness, it's a bit early, Patricia,' cautioned Verity, her face taking on an edge that chided me for wanting to drink before lunch and made me think my grand plan was already sunk. Then she sniggered, 'Only joking. I'll have a couple of gin and tonics too.'

I'd meant one each when I said a couple, but if she was going to make this mission easy for me then so be it. Mike gave a dutiful nod of his head, disappearing back toward the bar area, but getting stopped by other passengers wanting to place orders.

If Verity had noticed Mike tailing her at any point in the last few days, she gave no sign. Perhaps my boast that putting on the uniform made you invisible was proving to be true. It was certainly my experience and a smile creased my face as I thought back to my first adventure on the ship – dressing as a chef as I tried to catch the man responsible for killing Jack Langley.

'What are you thinking, Patricia?' Verity asked, catching me out. 'You have a wicked look on your face.'

'What? Oh, err, I was just thinking about what you asked me about my bodyguard.'

Now she leaned in, getting closer so we could whisper like conspirators, or perhaps more like cheeky schoolgirls given the ridiculous subject matter. 'Ooh, do tell,' Verity encouraged.

I gave a sorry smile. 'Nothing to tell, I'm afraid. I haven't seen him naked, and if anyone did, it was probably my Jermaine.'

Her forehead creased. 'What? You think he's gay?'

I shrugged, playing my part well, I thought. 'I don't know. I thought for a while that they might be flirting with each other.'

'Ugggh, what a waste,' Verity complained, slumping back onto her lounger. 'Why do you have a bodyguard anyway, Patricia? If you don't mind me asking. You're on a cruise ship. It seems like a fairly benign environment. Is there someone after you?'

And there it was. Without even having to manipulate the conversation, she was giving me an easy way to bring the subject up. My lips opened to start talking and froze. Why would she do that? Why would she invite me to talk about the bodyguard and his necessity? It felt like the spider was inviting me, the fly, into her house for tea.

I was staring at her with my jaw hanging open and about to get caught doing so when mercifully, Mike reappeared with the drinks.

'Oh, goody,' said Verity, bouncing off her lounger before I could react. 'Here you go, Patricia.' She offered me two balloon glasses of gin and tonic and I could tell by Mike's expression that she was giving me either one or both of the ones with alcohol in. How on Earth could I switch them now?

Verity plonked them into my hands – one for each, then grabbed her purse and swiped her card to pay for them. 'I'll get the first ones,' she grinned. 'I'm sure there'll be more yet.' Then, to my utter amazement, she grabbed the other two from the tray and downed eighty percent of the first in a single hit, gasping for effect and smacking her lips when she came up for air again. 'Come on, Patricia, this is good stuff.'

Seeing little choice as Mike scuttled away, I took a good glug from the glass in my right hand. It was Hendricks, my favourite, but my word it was strong. I had to focus my effort to not pull a face as I drank almost neat gin.

'I might go to the bar next time,' Verity announced with a scowl on her face. 'I don't think he put much gin in that one at all.'

'I'll go,' I replied quickly. 'It will be my round anyway.' I took another sip of my drink and tried to get my brain up to speed. Like a boxer in the first round, I was sizing up my opponent and looking for an opening to get a quick jab in. The door was open for me to talk about the Godmother. If I deliberately avoided the subject, how would I steer back to it later?

'I am being pursued, actually,' I announced. 'That's why I have a bodyguard.'

Verity almost dropped her drink in shock. 'You're kidding me,' she insisted.

'I wish I were.'

Doing a thoroughly convincing job of looking stunned by my revelation, Verity sat on her lounger, facing me with her feet on the deck. She was all ears. 'Why on Earth would someone be after you, Patricia?' she asked.

I eyed her drinks. The first was nothing but ice cubes melting in the glass and the second was in her hand. I could already feel the big hit of alcohol in my system and needed to get some in hers before the conversation was done.

Thinking fast, I downed the rest of my first glass and picked up the second. 'If I'm going to talk about that particular nightmare, I'll need some more of this,' I said, grabbing my purse with my free hand. 'I'll be back in just a minute.'

Verity looked a little taken aback that I was rushing off already; our first drinks arrived less than two minutes ago, but she said, 'Right, okay. I'll bet this is a juicy story then. I'll wait here.'

Good, she didn't suspect anything.

I sauntered causally to the bar, taking a sip of my drink just to confirm it was the same almost pure gin mix as the last one. Glancing around to see if anyone might be watching, I spat the sip back into the glass, and at the bar I poured it into a spill tray when the barmen were not looking.

'What can I get you?' asked a young man with an athletic physique and a handsome face; specially hand-picked to work in the pool area no doubt.

I glanced around again, looking for Mike quickly. 'If it's okay, I'll just wait for Mike to return. He makes them just the way I like,' I explained.

If my request surprised the barman, he showed no sign, moving along to attend to two pretty girls in their late teens instead.

Mike appeared a minute later, looking harried. 'This is harder work than I expected,' he complained. I was going to apologise, but he cut me off by adding. 'There are at least three people here that I have seen talking to the Godmother before.'

I almost turned my head to have him point them out but stopped myself before the obvious move gave us both away. 'Where are they?' I asked, my voice quiet.

Mike started making another four gin and tonics, talking as he did. 'I can't point them out, and if I do, your eye will then be drawn to them. I have Baker and the others watching them already. They are going to track them to their cabins and find out who they are. That will be important later. Were you able to switch the drinks?' he asked. 'I even positioned the tray so her drinks were on her side.'

I grimaced. 'No, I got both of the ones full of gin.' I watched him put four shots into one glass and then another and add none to the other two.

'Well, better luck this time then.' He placed the two non-alcoholic glasses on my side of the tray so I would be holding it with her drinks closest to her. She wouldn't be able to duck the alcohol this time.

Being careful with the heavy tray, and watching where my feet were going, I made it back to our loungers with her drinks facing toward her. She stood up to help me, rather than have me crouch down, which is when a ball shot out from the pool area and wiped out the two glasses on my side.

Ice-cold liquid, ice cubes and pieces of cucumber soaked the chest portion of my swimsuit, taking my breath away. Verity grabbed the two remaining glasses as swiftly as she could because I was moving about from the shock of it and threatening to drop the whole tray.

'Wow! Did you see that?' she squawked, levelling her eyes at the pool where an embarrassed dad was admonishing his two children. He jumped from the pool, rushing to my aid. 'I'm so sorry,' he blushed. 'I keep telling them not to throw it around. I'll take it off them now and deal with the stroppy behaviour that follows.'

'That's okay,' I spluttered, trying to put the tray down with the two upended glasses still rolling around on it and a small lake of spilled tonic swishing around. More of it spilled over the edge, getting my legs with its icy-coldness. 'It was just an accident.'

'Accidents can be avoided,' growled Verity, giving the man a cold stare.

I was beginning to feel sorry for him when he said, 'Um, there's a piece of cucumber in your swimsuit.' I glanced down to find a stick of the green fruit sticking out of my cleavage ... and he was reaching forward to pluck it out for me.

Reacting instinctively, my arms jerked upward to knock his hand away, which did the trick. Unfortunately, I was still holding the tray so the remaining tonic, plus ice-cubes and cucumber went into the air to then rain down on my head, showering me with freezing cold liquid.

Patricia Fisher, super klutz.

Verity and the dad both managed to dance back out of the way, leaving me gasping for breath with bits of ice and cucumber in my hair.

Verity's eyes could not be any wider. 'That looked bracing,' she commented, before bursting into laughter.

The dad, knowing he ought not to find my predicament funny, couldn't help himself and started laughing too. It was one of those times when it was a good thing I don't carry a gun. Otherwise ... well let's just say I wouldn't be stuck for targets. In the circumstances, I did the only thing I could and laughed too.

I was covered in tonic, which would be sticky once it dried, and the two alcohol-free drinks were gone again.

Verity handed me one of hers. 'Here, Patricia. You look like you need this.'

Inclined to agree, I took a swig and almost spat it back out – it was even stronger than the first one. Verity took a glug of hers too, smacking her lips together afterward. 'Ooh, that's better. Nothing like a decent portion of gin in one's tonic.'

The dad collected his ball, and with a final warning shout at his kids, gave it back to them. So much for dealing with their displeasure.

I used my towel to pat myself dry and picked the bits of cucumber from my hair. A steward, not Mike, came over with a dustpan and brush, tidied up the mess and took the tray back to the bar. Not doing very well in the getting-Verity-drunk stakes, I settled onto my lounger to regroup. I had yet another desperately strong gin and tonic ... might as well just call it gin given how strong it was. I would have to drink that, hope my constitution and regular gin drinking would see me fare better than Verity and try again in a little while. Maybe I could circle her back to the conversation about needing a bodyguard, but for now I wanted to ask her something else.

'How long have you kept a journal,' I asked, pointing at the ratty, old leather-bound book sticking out from her handbag.

Verity scowled at me. 'Oh, no you don't Patricia Fisher. You were just about to tell me all about having someone out to get you. I want to hear everything.'

Okay, so we were going to talk about her without mentioning her at any point. This should be fun.

I said, 'I don't really know how it happened.' Verity was all ears. 'I used to be a cleaner, you know that part already,' this wasn't our first conversation, 'but I never told you about how I came to be on the ship.' I launched into a preliminary story about finding Charlie with his pants down and my tearful flight to the ship. I told her about the missing sapphire which led into a discussion about Robert Schooner. She knew some of that story too because she was the one who killed him in the end.

The ironic part of our conversation was that I genuinely enjoyed talking to Verity. Yes, she is a deranged criminal overlord with an army of assassins and probably kills people every week just because they are in her way, but were it not for that, we might even be friends.

'Here you are, ladies,' said a steward, crouching between us with a fresh tray. 'Compliments of Mr Dowager for spilling your drinks earlier.'

Verity and I both glanced in the direction of the dad, who raised his own glass and made a sorry gesture yet again.

Perfect, another alcohol-filled drink.

Verity caught the steward's arm just as he was about to get up. 'Here, love, take these empties away with you.' She upended her previous glass and set it back on his tray then looked at me.

Bother. Verity and the steward were waiting for me to finish my drink. It was almost neat gin, but I drank it and handed the empty over, promising myself I would sip the next one. Verity had put away at least one stiff drink and had a second now. My head was beginning to feel a bit woozy, but I could still pull this off.

Once the steward departed, Verity asked, 'Now, where were we? Oh, yes. You were telling me about how you came to be on the ship and discovered an ability to solve mysteries. You were in Japan. That's where you got your dog, isn't it?'

And there it was – a little reminder that she wasn't who she said she was. I had never told her the story about the Yakusa and how I came to own Anna. Not wanting to tip her off about her little faux pas, I nodded, 'Yesh.'

Verity eyed me dubiously. 'Yesh?'

I felt my lips and moved my tongue around before trying again. 'Yes. That's what I meant to say. Apparently, that is where my current troubles really began. The bunch of mafia gangs from Miami, they were forgivable.'

Verity jinked one eyebrow to the sky. 'Forgivable? By whom?'

'The Godmother,' I replied, staring her dead in the face.

Her face was immobile for a moment before a laugh spluttered from her lips. 'The Godmother!' she roared. 'Oh, wow, Patricia! You really had me going for a while there. The Godmother.' She was howling with laughter. 'Let me guess: she is the head of an organised crime syndicate who deal with the fairies.' Her cackling was drawing attention from nearby passengers.

It was a strange way to react, making me question whether I had any of it right. Was she not the Godmother? Did I have it all wrong? I reached for my glass again and missed, my hand swishing through thin air twice before I managed to snag it on the second pass.

She calmed down a little, wiping tears from her eyes as she brought herself back under control. 'I'm sorry, Patricia. I know you just lost your butler and that he was a dear friend. It was cruel of me to laugh.' I had to watch as she wrestled her laughter into check and forced a more sombre expression onto her face. 'Whatever must you think of me?'

'Itsh, all right,' I slurred. 'Ferpectly fine. I would laugh too if I didn't know she wash real.'

'Patricia are you getting a little merry?' Verity asked.

My head was swimming from all the gin before lunchtime and thinking straight to deliver a sensible question was beyond me. 'I'm jushht going to put my head back for a moment.' I let her know.

Unable to stop myself, I fell asleep on the lounger, exposing myself to whatever the Godmother might want to do to me.

I could feel myself slipping away, too much alcohol forcing my body to shut down until it could recover, but I wasn't quite gone when I heard Verity's voice whispering by my left ear.

New Team Members

It was many hours later when I awoke to find I was in my bedroom back in the Windsor suite. As my eyes fluttered open, I sat up sharply, and instantly regretted it as the room swirled and my head pounded.

Sinking back into the covers, I felt the warmth of Anna and Georgie next to me. The dachshunds were cuddled up together in a tight little ball, radiating heat against my back. Judging that I was in no fit state to do anything else, I let sleep take me again.

The next time I came around, the clock by my bed told me it was almost three in the morning. The ship was at rest, that was the first thing my brain registered. It was due to dock in Glasgow at some point during the night and must have already done so. Carefully, I sat up in bed and gave myself a second.

I felt okay. Which is to say I had a mouth drier than a camel's ear in a sandstorm, an empty stomach from missing at least two meals, and a headache that would kill a ninja. I was in desperate need of water which, if Jermaine were here, would be in a pitcher on my nightstand. It wasn't but my phone was. Remembering something, I picked it up and checked. What I heard, chilled me to the bone. I found some clothes and quietly staggered to the kitchen. There I found water, drinking two pints just to get my body rehydrated, and went in search of some painkillers.

'Are you okay, Patty?'

Barbie's unexpected voice in the dark and quiet of the suite almost made me scream in shock. I thought I was being quiet, but Barbie had heard me rummaging around and was dressed ready for our usual night time rendezvous with the team.

Waiting for my heart to restart, I kept a hand on my chest and leaned on the kitchen counter for support. 'I need something for my head,' I murmured, the sound of my voice loud as it bounced off the inside of my skull.

'I bet you do,' said Barbie, going around me to find tablets in a drawer. 'Mike said you drank a whole bottle of gin.'

I groaned. 'I wore some of it.'

'So your skin was drunk too then,' Barbie concluded.

Sighing, I said, 'Me getting sozzled was not part of the plan. I intended to get Verity drunk and wheedle out of her something that would help us nail her.'

'Think you can manage to make it to Mike's?' she asked, starting toward the door. She was going with or without me.

Many sets of stairs later, because Barbie likes to get exercise in whenever she can, we arrived at cabin 34782 on deck eight. Mike answered the door, swinging it wide to show a full complement of secret agents inside.

'Hi, Mrs Fisher,' said Sam, my trusted assistant. He'd been enjoying a couple of days doing not much at all and spending time with his parents. The Downs Syndrome man of thirty ought not to be getting involved at all since he was still injured – Robert Schooner shot him – but he wanted to be a part of our mission, as he called it.

'Hi, Sam,' I waved back, looking around the room to see Alistair between his four lieutenants. Add Mike, Jermaine, Barbie and me to that and it still wasn't enough given that the Godmother had people on board.

I was going to try to even things up a little and it was time to tell those already present about it.

'I have some friends joining us,' I announced, taking a seat. 'I thought we could use a little extra help so I called in a few favours.'

'Who, Patty?' asked Barbie. Everyone else wanted to know too.

With a smile, I said, 'Well, for starters, there are two Hawaiians.'

Barbie blurted, 'Rick and Akamu! Those two troublemakers. Are they here in Scotland?'

My grin widened. 'Yes, they are. And if they are here ...'

'Mavis and Agnes must be with them,' concluded Jermaine.

Mike raised his hand. 'Who?'

There followed a few minutes of explanation as between me, Barbie, and Jermaine we retold some of the stories from the Aurelia and Zangrabar. Rick and Akamu were troublemakers but only in the sense that they were mischievous boys still hiding inside the skin of two men in their seventies. They were also ex cops and resourceful allies to have in any situation provided you didn't want them to move fast. A swift shuffle was their top speed.

Mavis and Agnes were two lifetime crooks from Ireland who had swindled, robbed, conned, and generally defrauded the rich people of the world to fund their own hedonistic lifestyle. They were wanted in most countries around the globe, but were also so good at forging, or finding the backdoor, that they never got caught. Even when they did find their way into a cell, they just let themselves out again. How the four got along given their polar opposite views of what law-abiding should mean was beyond me, but I guess they also stood testament that opposites attract.

'Anyone else I should know about?' asked Alistair warily. He wasn't a fan of Agnes and Mavis, largely because they had plagued his ship for weeks, stealing from his richest guests as they escaped one place and sailed to another. They had also played a large part in stopping a band of terrorists from killing everyone on the ship, so he was right to forgive them.

Jermaine asked, 'Is there anyone else, Madam?'

I knew the next person on my list was a special card in the deck. It made me want to blurt her name, but I spoke calmly and in a dignified manner as suited her character. 'Lady Mary Bostihill-Swank.'

'Oh, lord,' gasped Barbie. 'Are you going to try the drink-her-under-the-table routine on Verity again? Because with Lady Mary playing, it will probably work.'

My friend the socialite heiress, Lady Mary, was known to like a tipple or two ... for breakfast. By lunch the drinking began in earnest. I doubted she had been properly sober enough to drive since the nineties, but then she had a driver, and a helicopter with a pilot ... you get the general idea. She was seriously rich the day she was born and went on to marry a bestselling mystery/thriller novelist who made crazy money when compared to the average person. I felt a mild temptation to have Lady Mary pay Verity to leave me alone, but that would go against my policy on how to deal with bullies.

Alistair was looking at me, our eyes meeting across the room, as the others talked about the newest members of the team and what we might be able to do with their help. There was another person coming on board for certain, and a slim chance that one other might show up. The one for certain was to remain a secret for now, but only for a few hours. Alistair and I had been extra sneaky, but that was all to do with my future, and his. Or, I guess you might say ... ours.

I interrupted the conversation with a polite cough and took out my phone. I placed it down on the table and swung my eyes around the room to make sure I had everyone's attention. 'I'm sure you all know about my embarrassing failure to get Verity drunk earlier today.' I got several grins and a few sniggers in response. It was dark humour to cover the agitated worry we all felt. 'I was sober enough when I went into the gin swigging competition that I set my phone to record voice. It was on the table the whole time.'

Mike tilted his head to one side. 'I never noticed. When she left and the others dotted around the pool all went with her, I got Baker and his lot to grab a stretcher and carry you back to your suite.' That explained how I came to be back in my room, at least. 'I dropped your phone into your bag. Did it record anything interesting?'

Rather than answer his question, I leaned forward, opened the App, and pressed play. Verity's voice filled the room.

'I'm glad you didn't join in laughing, Patricia. I might have killed you right there and then if you had. It's been a long time since I killed anyone myself, you see. If things were different, you and I might even have grown to be friends, but you damaged my business and my partners and opponents expect me to deal with you as ruthlessly as they would.'

'It's nothing personal. Not really. I mean ... I recognise that you are an interfering, annoying busybody who wants to stop people doing the things they want to just

because they hurt other people, but that is the natural order of things. You are messing with God's natural order. That, as much as anything else, is why you have to die. It won't just be you though, Patricia. That's not the Alliance of Families' way. If you have children, they would be killed first. Your husband too, though in your case, I feel I would be doing you a favour by killing Charlie, so he gets a bye.'

'Instead, it will have to be your friends who help you pay the price for interfering. You could have saved them all by dying when I sent assassins after you. It's your fault they will go to their graves this week, just like that butler of yours.'

'Maybe, you heard some of this. Maybe you are unconscious and cannot hear a thing now. Were you trying to get me drunk, hoping I might leak something you could use against me? Poor, poor, Patricia. You never stood a chance.'

Around the cabin, eyes were wide, and no one was speaking. 'I had passed out by that point,' I told them all. 'I didn't get to hear it, but she clearly felt a need to gloat. She plans to kill anyone who she considers close to me and believes she has already taken care of Jermaine.'

Jermaine sniffed deeply. 'I note that she was careful to avoid admitting to anything.'

He wasn't wrong. 'We are dealing with a person who grew up in this environment. Someone who lives and breathes organised crime and has never operated on the right side of the law. Talking to me like that was a big slip for her. Possibly the biggest we are going to get.'

'Then how are we going to beat her, Mrs Fisher?' asked Anders Pippin.

I gave him the only answer I had, 'With luck.'

Chess Pieces

Before the sun was up in the morning, the ship was abuzz with excitement, the way it is each time the passengers arrive somewhere new. The feeling of anticipation is always greater when the ship has spent a couple of days at sea, which it had on the run across from Iceland.

The first thing I did, was send Verity an apology. In it, I made no mention of her whispered threats and the promises she made to kill my friends. I stifled a yawn, trying to keep my mouth from swinging wide open. I might have slept the afternoon and evening away, but it was false sleep, the type that you get when you are a bit tipsy ... who am I kidding, more like fully drunk in my case. Anyway, no quality comes from it, so when the team meeting went on for hours as we tried to work out a new strategy, I got hardly any sleep and I was tired now.

My message to Verity asked what she would be doing today and had she ever been to Glasgow before. I hadn't, which seemed shameful given how easy it was to get to from my home county of Kent – a person could drive there in a day easily.

No reply pinged immediately back, so I slipped my phone away to join Barbie on my suite's sun terrace. It was her first time in Glasgow though not her first time in Scotland. The ship had docked with our side facing the city, though in truth we were on the River Clyde which ran right through the centre of Glasgow. High rise buildings and ancient Scottish architecture flanked us whichever side of the ship one chose to look from.

'I have a surprise for you,' I announced, closing the terrace doors behind me to keep the warmth inside. 'And an acting job.'

She turned away from hanging over the railing and hitched an eyebrow. 'Oh?'

'Indeed. You should put your coat on. It will be cool on the dock.'

I didn't wait for her to question me; I went back inside to find my own warm gear which forced her to chase after me.

'Patty, what are you up to? You know I hate it when you get cryptic. Why are we going down to the dock? Is Verity heading into Glasgow? Are we going to follow her?'

With Anna and Georgie leading the way, and the silent Agent Garrett shadowing us, her questions continued all the way down the ship, to the royal suites' private exit. She was beginning to get annoyed with my refusal to tell her what I had in store when I led her off the ship and her questions stopped instantly.

The noise she made next was such a high-pitched, shrill scream that I had to believe I would need to accidentally nail one of my nipples to an escalator right before it vanished into the floor just to get anywhere near the same sound to come from my own body. Her arms flew into the air, and she ran. Fast strides carried her down the gangplank and onto the dock where a certain Japanese doctor waited.

I was smiling when I watched her leap at him, trusting that he would catch her when she landed with her legs wrapping around his middle. They hugged like that, Hideki holding her as she clung to him, and I made my way down to the dock to say hello. Anna and Georgie were straining at their leads: there was a human

41

they recognised and that meant treats or tummy scratches or a combination of both.

'Mrs Fisher,' Hideki nodded his head in acknowledgement.

Barbie scowled at me, but it was all in play. 'Ooh, Patty, you are a rotten friend. And you,' she swung a punch at Hideki's chest. 'Why did you lie to me? You said you couldn't get away from work.'

'Things changed at the last minute,' he lied again, catching my eye to confirm what she didn't know.

Barbie pulled him into another hug. 'Well, I'm glad they did. I missed you.' The last sentence was meant just for his ears, but I heard it too and knew I had made the right decision. Not only that, thanks to my impeccable timing, courtesy of a team of people watching her every movement, Verity and Walter stepped out of the regular passenger exit in time to see us.

I caught Verity's eye and waved, motioning that I would come to her in just a moment. 'Right you two, lovebirds. You need to make yourselves scarce.' I nodded my head back toward the royal suites' exit, just as Barbie gave me her confused face.

'Scarce? Why, what's going on?' she wanted to know. From the exit door and down the gangplank came two stewards, each holding two or more of Barbie's bags. 'You're sending me away?' Barbie asked. 'Is this because of the latest threat?'

'What latest threat?' asked Agent Garrett, speaking for the first time in over an hour.

Ignoring him, I said, 'Hideki will explain on the way.'

A Purple Star Cruise Line limousine pulled to a stop next to Hideki, and another steward, one dressed to be outside in the cool Scottish air, stepped up to the door to open it.

'But I want to stay with you, Patty,' Barbie argued. 'I know it's dangerous. That's the whole point, Patty. What if you need my help? What if there is a guard to distract? Who's going to ... to ...' she was grasping for a reason she was needed, 'to accidentally get their boobs out so he's looking the wrong way when we need him to?'

'What if he's a gay guard?' I countered. 'This is for the best, Barbie,' I assured her, pulling her into a hug. 'Let Hideki explain in the car.' Pulling her into a hug, I whispered, 'It's not what you think. Trust me and go with him. Remember to act like you are going forever, okay? We have an audience.'

I let her go and stepped back, creating space so she was nearer to Hideki and the car than to me. Finally getting that she needed to play along until she found out the rest of it, she dashed forward to pull me into a bearhug of a final embrace, then dived into the already loaded car.

When it pulled away, I didn't have to do much acting to make myself look sad.

Agent Garrett, not unusually, was eyeing me with deep suspicion. 'What are you up to, Mrs Fisher? Barbie didn't know anything about that did she? Is that her boyfriend? The doctor she is always talking about?'

I nodded. 'Yes. Did you not meet him at my house?'

Agent Garrett frowned at me, his face suggesting that he was trying to work something out. 'No. I think we passed in a hallway once. How come you just sprung that on her? She seemed completely thrown by it.' He knew there was something amiss but didn't know what it was. He wanted to be in charge, I knew that much already, and he made no secret of his desire to control my movements more closely. What really bugged him though, was me making decisions that made his job of keeping me safe more difficult and being in the dark about what I had planned ticked him off more than anything.

I patted his arm as I began making my way down the quayside to Verity. 'It was necessary to spring it on her. If I had let her know in advance, she would have resisted. Losing Jermaine was harder for her than for me in many ways. She would go to pieces if she were here for his ceremony today and that would do her no good. We all need to stay vigilant for the Godmother. I still think she might track me here.'

Wayne was still frowning. 'How could she possibly do that?'

'The Godmother?' I clarified. 'Can you be one hundred percent certain no one in your division of the police has been bought or coerced by her?'

He opened his mouth, intending to admonish me, but closed it again, letting his shoulder sag. 'Not one hundred percent, no,' he admitted.

'Very well then, Agent Garrett. Until you see any sign of someone targeting me, I guess I might as well enjoy my time in Glasgow.'

Getting closer to Verity, I made sure I looked suitably ashamed of the previous day. I wanted her to believe I had no idea of her true identity.

'What was that?' she asked as I got within speaking distance. 'That looked like your friend leaving.'

'Yes,' I replied, combining a shudder and a sigh with a smile. 'She's in love and she's been missing her boyfriend for too long. She belongs with him, not stuck on this ship with me.'

Verity's frown threatened to cleave her face into two pieces. 'She's leaving?' Her expression was pure thunder for a moment, and I got to watch her realise what I was seeing. Her smile reappeared so fast I found myself shocked it didn't hurt her face. 'When will she be back?' Verity asked.

'She's not coming back,' I told her with sadness etched into my voice. 'He's a doctor with a job in London and she can work anywhere. I hope to see them again after I return home. I think her real reason for going was Jermaine's death,' I revealed. 'She was here for him more than me. We were friends, but ...' I let my face crumble and moved into her personal space as I bawled, 'I feel so alone.'

I clung to her, giving her no option but to reciprocate the hug. 'There, there, Patricia,' she soothed. 'You still have Alistair and Sam. Plus your faithful bodyguard is always to hand. And you have me,' she concluded as I straightened myself again.

Verity's fake smile was still in place, but I could see the lack of emotional connection in her eyes. I patted her arm in thanks and stepped back. Agent Garrett held a handkerchief at arm's length for me to take. I used it to dab my eyes before handing it back.

I should have been on the stage.

Convinced that I had convinced her, I moved to the next item on my agenda. 'There is a small ceremony for Jermaine being held on the ship later this afternoon. I was hoping you might attend it with me.' Expecting her to try to decline, I pushed her, 'Please? It's just a short thing and Alistair will be giving it, so I won't be able to be with him. I just need a hand to hold.'

Unable to say no if she wanted to maintain her fake personality, she offered me a kindly smile and said, 'Yes, of course, Patricia. That's okay isn't it, Walter?' she asked without turning her head his way.

'S'pose,' he mumbled in his deep bass voice.

It was set then. If you are wondering what I am doing, the answer is a simple one: I'm trying to control her movements. She was going ashore today, something she hasn't done much, not that the ship has been anywhere but Reykjavik so far, but I took it to mean she had something she wanted to do in Glasgow and it probably involved her crime empire.

Looping my arm through hers and then through Walter's, like Judy Garland in *The Wizard of Oz*, but without the skipping and singing, I steered them away from the ship. At the royal suite's exit another limousine was waiting in case anyone needed it. 'How about we travel in style today? Where are we heading?' I asked, my voice filled with saccharine sweetness. I was imposing and I didn't care. Verity planned to kill me and my friends, but if the recording on my phone was anything to go by, she wouldn't move on me until she had dealt with everyone else. Knowing that gave me an advantage so I was going to remove the chess pieces from the board before she could eliminate them. That wasn't going to be easy though, I needed to do it in such a way that Verity didn't suspect anything.

On the spot and needing to name a destination, Verity grasped for a name. 'Um, Sauchiehall Street.'

I gave her a quizzical look. 'You're going shopping?' I might have never been to Glasgow, but I knew of its famous shopping precinct.

Struggling, but rallying, the Godmother wasn't going to let anyone put her on the back foot for long. 'Yes, Patricia,' she stated bluntly. It felt as close to a warning as she felt she could give while still pretending to be a sweet lady and friend. 'I thought I would treat myself to a few new bits. I expect they have sales on, everyone does these days.'

At the car, the steward stepped forward to hold the door. 'Good morning, Mrs Fisher,' he greeted me. 'Going anywhere nice today?' The limousine was angled away from us with the driver on the other side so none of us could see his face as we approached.

'To Sauchiehall Street for some shopping,' I beamed, getting in so I could see who was in the driver's seat. He and I locked eyes for the briefest second, then I bit my lip, once again acting my part. I had needed to get this close so I could check on something, but now it was done, I could back off. 'Goodness,' I blushed, backing out of the car once more. 'I've just realised how rude this is of me.' Verity could not have looked more confused in response to my latest statement. 'You're here on holiday as a couple and I am playing gooseberry. I'm such a tactless dummy some days. Please, go ahead. Take the limousine. I'm not really in a shopping mood anyway.'

Verity shot a glance at her husband, whose face betrayed no emotion at the change in plans. Looking back at me, she said, 'Well, if you are sure, Patricia.' Giving up so easily meant she didn't want me with her today, which was fine by me. I had other things to do.

I stepped back and showed her my sad smile again. 'I'm sure. I would just bring a sour note to your day.'

I watched the steward shut their door, and as they drove off, I gave a little wave before turning back toward the ship. I was smiling, but only to myself, keeping my secrets hidden.

Lieutenants Baker and Bhukari were standing guard at the royal suite's entrance, controlling people coming in and out though I knew they were not assigned to that duty today. They had stepped in momentarily so we could enact a ruse.

In the driver's seat of the limousine was Lieutenant Schneider. The real limo driver got a gratis day off so the tall Austrian could spy on the Godmother. He would drive them around for the day, monitoring where they went and who they met with. He had camera and video with him so would record their activities too. It was small, but it was a start. If they were here to meet organised crime people, Schneider would capture it.

I set it up a few hours ago when my head was clear enough to think straight. The guys quickly arranged a spare uniform so Schneider could play the role of chauffeur. If we were going to get her ... to get a law enforcement agency to believe we had identified the Godmother, then we needed plenty of evidence, not just a few pictures and videos. But, like I said, it was a start.

Agent Garrett travelled up in the elevator with me, heading for the top deck. It stopped on deck sixteen, the doors opening to reveal two men in the white uniform of the security team. They froze, both men staring at me with panicked eyes, then just as the elevator bonged for the doors to close, the leftmost went for his gun.

Gun Fight

Agent Garrett was already reacting when the bong sounded to warn passengers in the elevator car the doors were about to shut. With a yell brought on by a surge of adrenalin, he threw himself out of the doors, clubbing the handgun from the guard's hand. The gun skittered across the deck, but the sudden presence of a body between the doors broke the light beam that controlled the sensors and the doors reversed to slide open again.

That left me exposed with my bodyguard trying to fight two armed men. Not that I could have let the doors shut and left him, but what did I do now? Fear was making my body tense. Two seconds had passed, no more, and the second guard was now reaching for his weapon.

Agent Garrett was tussling with the first man. Unable to get to his own weapon tucked beneath his left arm, he would be an easy target for the second guard. I wanted to scream at them to ask what they were doing, but it was obvious: they had been bought by the Godmother.

From their surprised expressions, I felt certain they hadn't known we were in the elevator and hadn't been sent to kill me. Not yet at least. All that was moot now, of course, because it was life and death time.

I could feel myself shoving off the back wall of the elevator. The second guard was drawing his weapon, his right hand coming up from his belt, but I wasn't going to get to it in time. Not before he shot Wayne. A scream of rage escaped my lips.

And the two dachshunds came to the rescue.

The guards hadn't seen them, and it took the dogs a second or two to react. They were used to seeing humans and the ones in the white uniform they saw more often than any others. The security team and Alistair were always in my suite, and we saw them about the ship too. Also, the dogs were not trying to defend their territory i.e. my suite, so until they saw Agent Garrett, an extended member of their pack getting into a fight, they saw no reason to move.

Now though, they were two blazing streaks of noisy terror with teeth. Anna, no stranger to biting an ankle, sunk her teeth into the left leg of the second guard just as Georgie went for his right. With two dogs suddenly ripping into his flesh, the guard hopped back a step, his gun hand faltering as his brain and his nervous system fought for control of where to point it.

I smacked him in the face with my handbag. Okay, I get that it's a terrible cliché – the woman using her handbag as a weapon rather than punch a chap in the nose, but I don't have a lot of experience with hitting people and the handbag was right there.

It didn't have a lot of heft to it. It's not as if I chose to preload it for the occasion with a house brick. It did the trick though, catching him under the chin to snap his head back. Now he was really confused about what he needed to concentrate on, but he compensated for his confusion by pulling the trigger.

I screamed in shock, the sound of the shot making my ears ring. Behind me, the elevator bonged again, the doors shutting this time as the car went merrily on its way, oblivious that it might have cut off our best escape route.

Terrified to the point where it was all I could do to stop myself from just turning tail and running, I knew I had to disarm the guard before he managed to recover from the handbag uppercut and shoot me.

Then Agent Garrett hit him. He came from nowhere to deliver a clubbing downward blow from a high leap. It struck the guard on his chin, sending him crashing to the ground. Then, in one fluid motion, Wayne drew his gun and shot the guard twice in the chest.

Each shot was so loud in the small passageway that I felt the movement of air reverberate through my body. I was stunned. Rooted to the spot with fear and horror and revulsion.

'Why did you just shoot him?' I blurted the question as my startled eyes spotted the other guard, the one Agent Garrett tackled first, lying dead a few feet away. I hadn't heard Wayne shoot him, and then realised he couldn't have because I'd just seen him draw his weapon.

The second guard's wild shot had killed his colleague.

Wayne was breathing heavily, exertion and adrenalin placing heavy demands on his body in the space of less than thirty seconds. He staggered slightly, putting his left hand on his knee for support as he lowered himself to the deck to check the second guard's pulse. Only once he was sure the man was dead did he look my way.

'Why did I shoot him? Did you really just ask me that, Mrs Fisher? He had a gun in his hand, and he could have shot either one of us.'

I blinked a few times, arguing with myself inside my skull. The man had been on the deck. Better yet, the man had looked unconscious from the blow and the shooting looked more like a rage-fuelled execution than a defensive tactic to keep us both alive.

The back of my skull itched.

'Girls,' I called the dachshunds who were still worrying the dead guard's ankles. 'Girls, come here now.' They were still attached to their leads which I dropped the moment the action started. I stooped to collect them now, dragging the dogs away from the body and feeling exhausted as adrenalin faded away from my own bloodstream and made me feel spent.

Thumping footsteps were coming our way, announcing the arrival of ship's security, I hoped. However, looking down at the two men in their white uniforms, could I still see the security team as a safe haven?

Imposters

'Well, who are they then?' I wanted to know. I was back in my suite and feeling safe because I now had people I trusted around me. Alistair was yet to arrive because he was at the scene of the shooting, but I knew he would get to me as soon as he could. For now, I had Lieutenants Baker and Bhukari with me.

Lieutenant Bhukari said, 'We're working on that now, Mrs Fisher. What we do know is that they are not members of the Aurelia's crew.'

Lieutenant Baker was off to one side of the suite, talking on the radio as other members of the security detachment tried to find the identity of the two men.

Agent Garrett was sitting on one of the kitchen barstools while a medic inspected a wound to his ribs. It was sore, he claimed, playing it down but he'd been injured in his struggle with the first guard. Yet again he came to my rescue, defending me by putting his life on the line, but there was something ... off about what I had seen and I needed time to consider why I felt that way.

While my bodyguard was out of earshot, I dropped my voice to a hushed whisper and asked Deepa about Lieutenant Schneider. 'Has he reported back yet?'

She shook her head, keeping oral communication to a minimum. We had to be careful what we said in my suite because it was bugged. The team swept for bugs when I set in motion our secret squirrel club. They were going to remove them but doing so would tip our hand. More than that though, they gave us an excellent opportunity to feed false or misleading information back to whoever was listening.

Ultimately, that had to be the Godmother.

Just for the bugs, I said, 'I think they might be the Godmother's next attempt to kill me.'

Deepa sounded shocked when she replied, 'You think she tracked you here. How could she have?'

'She probably has people everywhere. They will be working as moles inside law enforcement agencies no doubt. There might be nowhere I am safe, but it definitely feels like I might be in danger here.'

'So, what will you do?' Deepa Bhukari asked on cue.

'It's time to wrap up my excursion and head somewhere else. Agent Garrett eliminated those two, but it won't be long before the Godmother sends more. That has been the pattern of it.'

We were establishing for anyone listening that we had no idea the Godmother was on board and watching me. From yesterday by the pool, Mike, Jermaine, and the lieutenants had tailed the people Mike recognised back to their accommodation. There were five in total, and we now knew who they were or, at least, the names on the passports they were using. We also knew where they were and could monitor th em.

The two men now on their way to the morgue were not among them, and it begged the question how many Verity might have with her. The vocalised threat that I would soon leave the ship and head elsewhere was to be a wakeup call to the Godmother. By offering her a dwindling timeline, I hoped to force her to step up whatever plan she had left. There was something else too, something I had noticed a while back but hadn't put much thought to until today.

Of course, with the suite bugged, I couldn't discuss it with anyone openly and would need to find some space and time away from Agent Garrett soon. I had a plan for that too. It was cruel, and might be unnecessary, but the two sides were playing for keeps and I couldn't afford to expose what I suspected to anyone I wasn't sure of.

Deepa asked, 'What will you do now, Mrs Fisher?'

Before I could answer, Lieutenant Baker came across to speak with us both. 'Neither man had any form of identification on them. Neither carried a wallet and at this point we are yet to identify even what cabin they were staying in. Their pictures will be circulated to the crew. Someone will recognise them.'

'What about their guns?' I asked.

Baker sighed a little. 'They are firearms from our own armoury. That they are missing from their stored location and not reported as such will raise some questions. The captain will be grilling people over this one. Their uniforms too are the real thing – spares taken from the store.'

It felt like time to throw in a curveball. I crossed the room to get to Agent Garrett. 'How is he?' I asked the medic.

'He's fine,' the medic replied, standing up and putting away his gear. 'The bruising,' which we could all see covering a foot-wide area on the left side of his ribs, 'is most likely the result of the ribs being dislodged. I've seen this happen before.

The fibres that sit between stretch and then tear, resulting in the bruising you can now see.'

Agent Garrett got to his feet and picked up his shirt. 'It's nothing, Mrs Fisher,' he assured me, but he winced as he moved his left arm to put the shirt on and would have sat back down on the barstool had we not been there watching him.

'It's clearly not,' I argued. 'Perhaps you should rest. I don't need to go anywhere.'

I got the suspicious eyes from him again. 'Really, Mrs Fisher? That's usually what you say right before you set off on an adventure.'

'Okay,' I put my hands up in defeat. 'I want to look into a spate of robberies on board the ship; the ones we were talking about earlier.' His brow furrowed. 'I won't leave the ship and I will have Baker and Bhukari by my side at all times. Isn't that right?' I prompted.

Caught on the hop, Lieutenant Baker said, 'What? Oh, err, yes. Absolutely, Mrs Fisher.'

Deepa Bhukari rolled her eyes. 'We could do with the help actually.'

Wayne's brow hadn't straightened itself out yet. 'Aren't Hamond and Zaki on it?'

He wasn't wrong. 'Yes,' I replied, 'but they are not getting anywhere, and I need something to distract myself with before Jermaine's ceremony later.'

Clearly in pain, otherwise he would never have considered letting me out of his sight, Agent Garrett said, 'You promise to stay with your security and to stay on the ship?'

I made the Girl Guides salute, holding three fingers of my right hand up by my right shoulder. 'I promise.'

It was Wayne's turn to roll his eyes. 'I think I'll come along anyway. You'll just have to go slow.'

Bother.

My plan to lose him was failing already, and now I had committed myself to looking into the odd robbery cases. Accepting my position, because fighting it would arouse Agent Garrett's suspicion (and he was suspicious enough most of the time anyway), I asked Lieutenant Baker, 'Where can I find Hamond and Zaki?'

Hypnotism Doesn't Work

I left Anna and Georgie in my bedroom where they had a bed and water and access to their doggy toilet. I liked having them with me but, if I'm being honest, dachshunds are really lazy, and Anna would start complaining if I made her do too much.

We found the two Lieutenants in a cabaret bar on the eighteenth deck where they were exploring the idea that the confused couple I'd met two nights ago, and all the previous victims, had been hypnotised.

'Hypnotised?' Sam repeated. I'd chosen to collect him on the way down since I knew from Melissa they had chosen to stay on board today. Paul had eaten something which didn't agree with him, forcing regular visits to the smallest room, and she had spent a term at a University in Glasgow in her early twenties and wasn't fussed about seeing it again.

Zaki frowned at Sam's contorted face, not liking the disbelief he saw there. 'Hypnotism is a real thing,' he insisted.

'No, it isn't,' argued Hamond. 'It's a load of fake mumbo-jumbo. Only crazy people like you believe in it.'

Taken aback by the insult, Zaki rounded on his partner. 'Are you saying something about my religious and ethical beliefs?'

Lieutenant Baker stepped between them. 'I think we'll just park that discussion for now, shall we? What led you to believe they might have been hypnotised?'

'It was a matter of deduction,' boasted Hamond proudly. 'Not the hypnotism part,' he corrected himself quickly. 'But when we interviewed the victims again, we discovered they had all attended this hypnotism act the evening they were robbed and they were all people who volunteered to take part in the show.'

'The obvious conclusion being,' Zaki interrupted to make his point, 'that the hypnotist kept them under. When he left here each night, he then went on to rob the victims, instructing them to forget the experience or that it was him. That is why they are so fuzzy on what happened.'

Hamond rolled his eyes and I got the impression they had been over this back and forth for some time. Rather than restart the argument, Hamond said, 'The hypnotism act is the only correlating or linking factor we have been able to find. I wanted to check the place out, have a look around and such ... just to familiarise myself with it. Next, we were going to take a trip to see the hypnotist.'

Baker cut his eyes at me, asking my opinion on their crazy theories.

I shrugged. 'It's as good a place to start as any.'

The small theatre could hold maybe a hundred people at a push which had to make it one of the smallest venues on the ship. It wouldn't open for hours but behind the bar two men were working. They had on the usual black trousers, shirt, and apron of the bar staff around the ship, their shirts accented by a Purple Star Cruise Line's motif on the collar. They were restocking the optics and performing other mundane admin tasks, going about their business with no interest in what we might be doing in the club in the middle of the day.

Everyone started to move toward the door, except me, as I chose to look around and familiarise myself with the cabaret bar. It wouldn't occur to me to attend a hypnosis act because I was certain it was exactly that. I didn't want to be investigating this case at all, but now that I was, I not only needed to do so in a manner that would convince Agent Garrett, who also had not moved to the door as he waited for me, but I also figured I might as well do it properly.

Turning to leave, I caught sight of the flyer on the wall displaying a handsome man in his late fifties, a head of grey hair made him look quite dashing despite the purple cape and almost naked female assistant seemingly levitating for him.

'William Controller,' Agent Garrett read aloud and smirked. 'Will controller. That's a good one.'

I might admit it was original, but the tortured play on words did nothing to impress me. Outside, Lieutenant Zaki was giving the team pointers on how to avoid getting hypnotised.

'That's what I'm telling you, man,' he whined at Hamond. 'No one ever thinks it's the hypnotist because he hypnotises you into thinking it must be someone else. Think about it. If we know he's the robber, we go in there and try to arrest him, and BAM! He goes and pulls a whammy on us and we spend the rest of the day thinking we are chickens or something.'

Hamond wasn't buying a word of it. 'Zaki you have got more than one screw loose. You need to submit yourself for psychiatric testing because I'm not sure it's safe to have you wandering around armed all the time.'

'Just remember to not make eye contact,' Zaki warned. 'And if you do, or if you need to, make sure you don't hold it for more than a few seconds.'

'How many seconds would be safe?' asked Sam, who might be wondering if this was real, or might be pulling Zaki's leg.

Zaki took the subject deadly serious, sucking in a breath between his teeth as he thought about his answer. 'I don't know. Maybe five or six would be safe enough. Ten would be too many though.'

'Or we end up squawking like chickens, right?' Hamond tried to confirm in a deadpan voice.

Zaki narrowed his eyes. 'You think this is a joke? My Auntie Shadia, she went to a hypnotist to get him to stop her smoking. She quit the same day and never had another one as long as she lived.'

'How long did she live?' Hamond wanted to know.

Zaki went a little red. 'Two days. She got knocked down by a runaway camel.' A laugh burst from Hamond's lips and I had to bite down my own snort of amusement. Annoyed, Zaki snapped, 'But that doesn't change anything. Those two days were cigarette free and she swore it was all down to the hypnotist.'

His jabbering saw us all the way down to the crew decks where we found the hypnotist's cabin. It was on the sixth deck, where the higher-ranking crew had their cabins. They were fifty percent bigger which always struck me as strange – why would getting promoted mean you need more space? I guess it was a reward thing, something to make the lower ranks want to climb the ladder of success. Personally, it made me feel uncomfortable because it segregated the crew into have and have-nots. Worried that my thoughts might sound a little communist, I kept them to myself.

A knock on his door, Hamond using his knuckles, caused a deep, theatrical voice to say, 'Pray enter,' then the door swung smoothly inwards to reveal Will Controller standing in the centre of his room. His accent was hard to place, the theatrical emphasis he used distorting it but English was his first language in my opinion.

'Oh, my Lord,' gasped Zaki. 'How did he open the door? He's nowhere near it.'

The answer was soon revealed when his assistant, still wearing almost nothing, stepped out from behind the door.

Next to me Zaki let go a breath he'd been holding, and Sam's eyes almost popped out of his head at the attractive, bronzed woman with the ridiculously inflated breasts. Her bikini top was little more than two triangles that covered her nipples and her boobs looked like two balloons just hanging around defying gravity while attached to her chest. Some men might go in for that look, but I couldn't for the life of me imagine why.

'Close your mouth,' I whispered in Sam's ear as I passed him.

Will Controller was wearing his full stage outfit complete with cape, and his room was filled with candles that backlit him and provided all the light in the cabin. The candlelight also gave the man a macabre appearance, lighting his face from below in an eerie way. It made me question whether what he had in fact said was, 'Prey, enter.'

Lieutenant Baker flicked on the lights. 'You know you're not allowed candles down here. What were you thinking? This endangers everyone.' He carried on around the cabin, stubbing the candles out as if the space were his.

If Baker's telling off bothered him, it didn't make it to Will Controller's face where his dangerous and spooky edge remained in place. 'They are a necessary element of the show. It would be improper to rehearse without them. Why are you here?' he demanded to know.

Zaki stumbled into the cabin, shoved over the threshold by Hamond who now bore a wicked grin at his colleague's expense. Poor Zaki looked genuinely spooked, his eyes darting all around the cabin as he took in props such as a poster of an eye captured inside a pyramid and a holographic photograph of the hypnotist on one wall which opened and closed a third eye in the centre of his forehead depending on what angle one viewed it from.

Hamond said, 'Go ahead, Zaki. Tell the man why we are here.'

Sam got there first. 'To arrest you for hypnotising people so you can rob them,' he supplied with a broad grin.

Will Controller hiked an eyebrow.

With a sorry sigh, Lieutenant Baker took over. 'Sir, we have reason to believe multiple victims of robbery have attended your act either immediately or shortly before the crime was committed. We are following up on that lead and wanted to start with you.'

'You thinkest me to be the criminal, using my powers for dark means?' It wasn't quite a roar when he questioned what Baker might or might not believe, but it carried a lot of indignation. 'I once played the Palladium,' he complained, naming the most famous stage in London.

'But you don't play there anymore,' I pointed out, involving myself because Agent Garrett was watching and that was what I would usually do. 'However, I don't believe any of us are accusing you of anything at this time. The fact that all the victims came to your act before being robbed suggests the guilty person might be in your audience each time.' Having established that we were not there to levy blame at his door, I saw him visibly relax.

'But the victims were always in a confused state,' blurted Zaki, making everyone look his way. He quickly cast his eyes down to the carpet, avoiding looking into the hypnotist's eyes lest he fall instantly under his spell. 'They were confused and disoriented, just as if they had been hypnotised.'

'Not possible,' Will Controller assured us all.

Lieutenant Bhukari challenged him, 'How so?'

'Because it's all a load of fake rubbish,' snapped his assistant, speaking for the first time and grabbing a chair from a nearby table so she could plonk herself into it. Her accent was one I did recognise, it was from the south east of England – my home turf, where residents in the big cities such as Maidstone were apt to talk in a common manner.

Will gave her a crestfallen look. 'Come on, love,' he pleaded, his posh accent abandoned so now he sounded just like her. 'We agreed to keep the act up at all times in public.'

'What happened to his voice?' asked Sam.

I explained, 'He's an actor, Sam. They both are. Part of their act is to look and sound right for the part.'

'Yeah,' said Miss Balloon Chest the Assistant. 'It means,' she switched back to the plum in mouth voice, 'always talking like a complete idiot.'

She was glaring at him and he was getting angry with her and the whole thing was about to explode into an argument. Lieutenant Baker could see it too, stepping between them much like he had with Zaki and Hamond earlier.

'I think we should interview you both separately, yes?' It was phrased as a question, but there was no option to disagree. Lieutenant Baker was taking control of the situation, showing his leadership ability and dominance. I caught the lustful look in Deepa Bhukari's eyes as she listened to her fiancé give out instructions. It was Will's cabin, his assistant, Tammy-Jo, had a smaller cabin on deck four, so she was to go with Zaki and Hamond while we stayed here to speak with the hypnotist.

Despite the couple admitting the act was nothing other than that, Zaki still looked relieved to escape. They were taking her to one of the security team rooms a few decks up. 'Do you want to put something else on?' I asked her, thinking more about public decency than her personal comfort.

She paused in the doorway. 'Sure, you're right. Can you pass me that robe, sweetie?' Her question was addressed to Sam, who obediently, and with eyes still on stalks, grabbed the garment she pointed to. It was a sheer, turquoise thing that I could have folded up and put in a pocket without noticing it was there. It was so short it failed to cover her bum cheeks.

Nevertheless, she tied it around her waist as if it made a big difference and tottered through the door on her six-inch spike heels. I placed my hand on Sam's head and turned him through one hundred and eighty degrees so he wasn't salivating at her back.

Now, where were we?

'Have you noticed anyone repeatedly appearing in your audience?' I asked.

All trace of his fake accent was gone when he replied, 'Nah. To be honest, I don't pay much attention to them. The whole thing is a con.'

'Don't you get volunteers from the audience?' asked Deepa confirming what I expected to be the case from my limited exposure to the art.

Will, whose real name we now knew was Kevin Plumley, nodded his head vigorously. 'Oh yeah, absolutely. We ask for volunteers because that is what a lot of them come along for. They come up to the front as a group and I hypnotise them. Inevitably, hypnotism doesn't work on the real volunteers which I explain away by buttering them up a bit with statements like, "Some are just too strong willed to be controlled". The audience has two ringers, Brenda and Liam. They are the ones who play the fool, keeping the audience entertained by doing all the daft things

I ask them to. Of course, we always get some from the audience who choose to pretend to be hypnotised as well. I love hearing them when they go back to their friends or family, claiming they really were hypnotised and then lying that they had no idea they had just pretended to be Michael Jackson singing *Thriller*.'

Lieutenant Baker interrupted his flow. 'Okay, so we've established your show is a load of hokum, but three couples have been robbed after attending the show. In each case, they have been, as Lieutenant Zaki said, disorientated and confused and claimed to have been volunteers who took part in your show. None of them were able to give a description of their attacker or provide a clear account of what had happened. None had been violently assaulted in the thefts and it would seem they willingly gave their possessions over when instructed to do so. If it's not you hypnotising them, then what is going on?'

Worrying Thoughts

It was lunch time when we made it back up from the crew decks none the wiser for our preliminary investigation. The passengers disembarking to explore Glasgow would all have gone ashore by now and those joining the ship would be mostly aboard already. That meant I had people to see, but just like with everything else, I had to lose Agent Garrett to do so.

I wanted to bring him into the fold, I truly did. He would be an excellent ally to have included in our secret squirrel club, but there was something holding me back and it wasn't just his affiliation with law enforcement agencies who could contain leaks. There was something else now and it started when he shot the guard earlier. I had been in a state of shock, so maybe he was right, and the man was just about to fire his gun. But what if I was right, and there had been no danger? We could have grilled him for information. He might have been our way to get an angle on the Godmother. To my knowledge, they were yet to work out who either of the dead men were and that was because Agent Garrett had killed the second man.

My skull itched again, trying to tell me something.

'Are we getting lunch now, Mrs Fisher?' asked Sam, popping the bubble of thoughts above my head.

It was about time I ate something since breakfast was many hours behind me. Could I combine that task with losing Agent Garrett? I shot Sam a smile. 'It certainly is. Do you want to have lunch with your mum and dad?'

He shook his head vigorously. 'No, Mrs Fisher. Mum and dad are no fun. They always want me to eat a salad or something with vegetables in it, and dad is sick anyway.'

I chuckled at him. I guess I was the fun one who paid no attention to what he ate. He wasn't my child, and he was, despite the Downs, a grown man able to make his own decisions. He earned his own money as my assistant so who was I to dictate how he spent it? Besides, I would normally have lunch with either Barbie, or Jermaine. Or, more recently, Alistair. Agent Garrett rarely spoke so wasn't much of a lunch companion. At least Sam was funny.

We picked a place on deck eighteen, a burger bar, because that was Sam's choice and the simplicity of a hot sandwich and some salty fries appealed to me. Tucking into our food and the lack of conversation it brought gave me a chance to think. My phone had pinged several times in the last hour, each text message a confirmation that a different person, or group of people were aboard. I needed to meet with them. I needed to get messages to them at the very least. I couldn't do that without Agent Garrett seeing them, and worse yet, he met Rick, Akamu, and the girls in London so would spot them if they came into sight anywhere on the ship.

I needed a way to ditch him, and just like that, a simple way to do it popped into my head with a big fat why-didn't-you-think-of-this-earlier on the side. Mopping up the last of my fries and using a napkin to wipe the grease from my fingers, I sent a quick text and then announced my plan for the rest of the afternoon.

'I am going to take myself to the spa.' Agent Garrett couldn't respond straight away because I had waited for him to take a bite of his burger before I spoke. 'I'm too distracted by Jermaine and I feel like the ceremony later is hanging over my head. I need to just get away for a while and detach myself. The spa sounds like the perfect way to do that.'

The Aurelia being a luxury cruise ship, the most luxurious cruise ship on the planet in fact, at least that is what the cruise line continually bragged, there was more than one spa. I hadn't been in all of them, but I was willing to bet they were all amazing. There was one in particular that I favoured though, and it was where I would be pretending to spend the next few hours simply because it was ladies only.

Agent Garrett cleared his mouth. 'You're not going to pursue the strange hypnosis robbery case?' He'd been around me for a couple of weeks now and had learned, or more accurately borne witness to, my incessant dogged pursuit of the truth once I had my teeth into a mystery. Not doing so now was out of character, but I was fine with that.

'I will take the quiet time to contemplate what I have seen,' I told him. 'But otherwise, no. I think what I need more than anything, is some me time.'

He pursed his lips and looked unhappy about my decision. 'Alright then, Mrs Fisher. I shall escort you to the door and will wait outside until you are finished. I'm guessing you intend to visit the ladies-only spa on deck nineteen.' He was smarter than I gave him credit for.

'What should I do, Mrs Fisher?' asked Sam.

I thought it testament to how capable Sam was that he'd not once let slip anything in Wayne's presence that might tip him off to the secret goings on Sam and I were involved in. Everyone overlooked him as if his condition made him less of a person. He was asking me for guidance, but as his employer I expected that.

I leaned in to whisper in Sam's ear with a conspiratorial wink at Agent Garrett. 'Take yourself to Mike's cabin when we leave here and help them with surveillance. Just don't let Agent Garrett know that's what you are doing.'

My wink and grin disarmed Agent Garrett, like most, he paid little attention to Sam and totally underestimated what the man was capable of. I paid and tipped our waiter, gathered my things, and started for the door. In truth, an afternoon of relaxing in the spa sounded heavenly, and I made a mental promise to do just that with a couple of ladies once this was over. I could feel it drawing to a close, but the question now came down to who would blink first. I knew who Verity was, but did she suspect that I knew? Would I cave and accuse her because I thought she was about to do something heinous? Or would I let slip something that let her see that I wasn't fooled? I wanted to be the one to spring it on her, and that meant we were entering a cagey game because she could reveal herself at any time, most especially if she felt threatened. I was trying to draw a net in around her, and though I was still weaving the net, if I can stretch the analogy that far, I could see it in my mind. Would I catch her, or was she wilier than I thought?

That was probably my biggest concern and it preyed heavily on my mind as we made our way back to the escalator. I felt like I was winning. Very slowly, yes, but winning, nevertheless. But what if she already had someone inside my team and they were telling her everything? What if she were just far cleverer than I thought and was about to spring a trap on me. I couldn't see it coming, that was for sure. Would the game end with my death just the way she wanted?

The thought made me gulp loud enough for Agent Garrett to turn his head and look my way.

The Spa

As promised, Agent Garrett escorted me to the spa and came just inside the door to the reception area which was as far as he was permitted to go. There were large signs up boldly insisting no men go beyond that point.

From my bedroom in the Windsor suite, I'd sent a text message to my Hawaiian friends, finally acknowledging their message, and letting them know I had complications and would endeavour to be with them soon. I knew where they were because Alistair arranged the cabins on my behalf. I wanted my A-Team to be together geographically and far away from anywhere where I might accidentally run into Verity, Walter, or anyone else from her side.

So far, we had identified seven probable henchmen and women ... should that be henchperson? I often struggled with what was now PC with women and men moving into roles that have been traditionally dominated by one gender or the other. I decided to label them as bad people and move on. They were dotted about the ship, and it was nothing other than God's grace that none were located near to Mike's cabin on the eighth deck. So that was where we put everyone else. Lady Mary wouldn't be enthralled by that arrangement but if there was a regular supply of gin, she would probably sleep on a couch.

'You know, Wayne,' I said just before Patrice, my masseuse, led me through to the spa proper, 'I will be in here for three hours. Maybe you should head back to the suite and rest. I don't think anyone will try to get me here.'

He gave me a dry look. 'Mrs Fisher, there is no need to concern yourself with my well-being. My task is to keep you safe. Right now, that means watching the door to the spa and making sure no one goes through it that I don't like the look of.' He switched his attention to the lady manning the reception desk. 'Is there another way out of here? An emergency exit?'

'Of course,' she replied, surprised at the question and probably the forceful tone with which it was asked. 'It sets off an alarm if anyone touches it though, so don't worry. If it sounds, you will know about it.'

He puffed out his cheeks slightly and exhaled through his nose, an act I'd seen him perform countless times when he was trying to reach a decision. After a two-count, just when I was going to abandon him to go with Patrice, he said, 'Okay.' He left, heading back out the door to wait for me.

Patrice said, 'Goodness, he's intense.'

The moment the door swung shut, I blurted, 'I need your help. You've got to help me get away from him.'

The two ladies looked at each other, confused and quizzical looks fighting for dominance, but when they turned back to face me, I could tell they were going to help.

'What do you need us to do?' asked Patrice.

I couldn't go out through the emergency exit which would return me to the deck around the corner in a different passageway. If I did that, the alarm would go off and Agent Garrett would guess it was me.

'But there's no other way out,' said Faye, the lady from reception as I led them through the spa. I'd been in here before, so I knew there was another exit. It wasn't exactly conventional, and it certainly didn't say exit, and it didn't even have a door as such, but when I stopped walking, both the ladies with me knew what I had planned.

Patrice's eyes were bugging out as she looked up. 'You must be crazy!'

I was ready to second her opinion. The nineteenth deck lady's spa extended to the edge of the ship where a sun terrace provided a place for their hydrotherapy treatments. The hot and cold bathing system was supposed to energize and rest the body, improving blood circulation and activating the lymphatic system to help detoxification. It also actively promotes the release of endorphins. At least, that was what the blurb in the brochure said. I wasn't crazy enough to find out by immersing myself in near-freezing water and neither was anyone else because the terrace was empty.

The point is, I was now outside. All I had to do was go up or down and I would find another balcony. However, to do either thing I had to climb over the balcony and hang over the side of the ship. It was a long way down to the Clyde river beneath me.

I stuck my head over the side and craned my head around to look up.

'Good afternoon, madam,' said Jermaine, giving me a wave from the cabin above. Since I was on the nineteenth deck and above me was the top deck, the cabin directly above was one of the ship's palatial suites. All the best suites came with a butler and Jermaine, being the butler in the grandest suite of them all – mine – knew all the other butlers.

Another head popped out next to Jermaine's, this one belonging to the butler of the suite, I guessed. I could only see his head, but he had that butlery look about him.

Jermaine called down, 'Stand aside, madam. I shall throw you the rope.'

Rope?

I was hoping for a full climbing rig complete with safety harness and helmet. He wasn't lying though because what arrived with a soft thump dangling down from the deck above was a rope. There was a loop in it for me to put my foot in.

Patrice came to the edge of the terrace and looked down. 'You must be crazy,' she repeated. 'Ain't no way, I would go out there.'

The concept didn't enthral me either but going out there was only the half of it. I had to come back down later so Agent Garrett would see me coming out of the spa via the same door I went in through.

My legs were shaking as I grabbed the rope. This had been my idea, no one else's. A quick message to Jermaine from the burger bar was all it took to make the arrangements, my butler demonstrating his ability to get things done quickly by being ready before me.

With both hands on the rope, I stepped onto the edge of the balcony. Faye rushed forward, 'Don't just stand there, Patrice. Give me a hand to help keep her steady.' The two ladies helped me to keep my balance so I could get my legs into position and get one foot into the loop.

This time when I looked up, I saw Mike looking back down at me. When he saw me looking, he held out a warning hand telling me to stop.

'What is it?' I begged him urgently. There was a chill breeze blowing through and I was dressed for an afternoon at the spa. Also, I was terrified and beginning to doubt I could keep my shaking legs locked while they hauled me up.

'Just a second, Patricia,' he called back down. 'We're just checking the breaking strain of the rope.'

I opened my mouth to say, 'Okay,' and then realised what the cheeky git had said. Before I could retort, the rope started moving, lifting me into the air and away from the side of the ship. People on the other side of the river would be able to see the daredevil stunt taking place but because we were on the side facing the river, the passengers and crew on the dock couldn't see a thing.

Too scared to speak, I flashed Faye and Patrice a tight smile just before my head vanished from their view.

Above me, Mike was looking down, relaying my position to the people in the suite doing the hard work. 'It's heavier than they expected,' he shouted. 'What did you have for lunch?'

I was going to smack him in the trousers if he wasn't careful. I understood what he was doing though – my mind wasn't on the terrifying drop to the cold water beneath me, it was on him and his smart mouth.

Fearing for my life, holding on so tight it hurt my hands, and forcing myself to relax my clenched teeth because it was starting to make my jaw ache, I heard the sound of a helicopter going overhead. Looking up, all I saw was a flash of something shiny going by before it was eclipsed by the ship's superstructure. I could guess who was on board.

Another two heaves and my fingers touched Mike's. On the next one, my head popped above the edge of the terrace and hands were grabbing me. I just had to negotiate the balustrade and get my feet back onto the deck and I would feel safe again. Lieutenants Baker and Pippin were there, along with Jermaine and Sam and Mike and the suite's butler. They had rigged the rope around a column in the suite and bodily hauled me using brute strength. They were all breathing heavily. All except Mike that is who was still chuckling to himself about getting away with so many insults, and Jermaine, who had his arm in a sling still and wasn't able to take part.

As hands began to pull me, I saw the security of the terrace and threw myself forward. However, my foot got caught in the loop of the rope, which came with me, the rope looping around Pippin and Baker as they tried to help. Yanked away by the unexpected tug, their hands were suddenly not there to catch me, and I toppled.

Mike tried to grab my upper body, but I slipped through his arms as I somersaulted over the edge of the terrace balustrade and onto the floor. I was on the deck and I was safe, but I really didn't feel like doing that again in reverse.

'Madam, are you all right?' asked Jermaine, kneeling by my side to help me up with his one good arm.

Decorum would not allow me to admit that I jolly near wet myself, so I said, 'Yes, thank you, Jermaine,' and let him help me to my feet. Once up and certain my feet were steady, I looked around to see everyone else. 'Thank you all, gentlemen. That was most … exhilarating. Now, I'm against a running clock and I'm sure you all want to get back to what you were doing.' I had interrupted most of them as they stalked/followed the men and women thus far identified as probable agents of the Godmother.

Jermaine, who was rarely seen wearing clothing other than his butler's livery or a splendid suit, was today adorned in a garish t-shirt, board shorts, and had a head of fake dreadlocks coming from beneath a hat. If I didn't know it was him, I would pass him in a passageway and never think to look twice. I guessed it was also easier to don with one arm in a sling.

No one knew about Mike, and the lieutenants were in uniform which made them mostly invisible as they moved around the ship. I also knew the chaps were taking it in turns to tail different people so, if the Godmother's bad people were being vigilant, they would not keep seeing the same person.

'Were you able to obtain a uniform?' I asked before they dispersed.

'I have it in the guest bedroom, madam,' said the suite's butler.

Addressing him, I said, 'Thank you ...'

'Victor, madam,' he supplied.

'Yes. Thank you, Victor.'

Without further ado, we set about our tasks. The chaps headed for the door while Victor removed the rope. Lieutenant Baker hefted it over one shoulder and left with it. I just had to hope the passengers staying in the suite did not return before I needed to descend again. I went into the bedroom hoping to find a set of steward's clothing. My plan was to pass unnoticed around the ship by wearing a disguise. Wayne might get up to stretch his legs, the Godmother's agents might spot me as they roved around the ship ... after this morning's gunfight I had no desire to wander the ship alone, but that was what this current situation called for and I did not wish to be spotted.

I didn't find a steward's uniform though, I guess they couldn't find one my size in the tiny timeframe I gave them. Instead, I had the pure white uniform of a security officer complete with lieutenant's insignia on the epaulette. It would have to do. I changed in a hurry, laying my own clothes out on the bed so they wouldn't crease, but what to do about my hair? The female crewmembers either wore their hair short or tied it up. Mine hung beneath my shoulders and I had nothing about my person or in my handbag that I could use to fix that. Wriggling my lips left and right as I stared in the mirror, all I could come up with was hanging my head upside down and stuffing the hat on to trap all the hair inside.

To achieve that I laid on the bed so my head was off the side. It took a couple of attempts, but I got all but a few wisps which I stuck down with a splash of water from the bedroom's adjoining bathroom.

Ready to go, I thanked Victor again, made a note of the suite number on the way out, and hurried away to the roof.

Slumming It

The person in the helicopter was Lady Mary Bostihill-Swank. She was the kind of woman who if asked if she were the richest person in England would give an aghast look and say, 'Goodness, no. Whatever gave you such an idea. I'm fourth, I think.'

She owned a wildlife park in my home county of Kent which did a year-round roaring trade, no pun intended. I suspected there were many other strings to her bow, but finance is not the sort of thing one discusses.

I met her as she was coming down from the helipad. 'Lady Mary,' I hallooed her with a wave.

'Ah, yes. If you could just give the stewards a hand with the bags, there's a good fellow. One never knows how much to pack for these little trips.' She hadn't recognised me at all, which was a compliment to my disguise, but unhelpful, nevertheless.

I barred her way, folding my arms and standing my ground until she bothered to make eye contact with my face.

'Goodness, Patricia, is that you?' she gasped when her brain finally cottoned onto the message her eyes were sending. 'I didn't know you had joined the crew.' Her grin turned saucy. 'Is this just so that captain of yours can administer appropriate punishment?' she asked while miming a smack on the bottom.

I felt heat in the cheeks. 'Heavens no, Mary. I'm in disguise so the Godmother's people won't notice me if they walk by.'

Struggling down the stairs behind her, two stewards were grunting and straining under the load of bags they had to carry.

Spotting them, Lady Mary wrinkled her brow. 'They really ought to think about putting in an elevator down from the helipad.' She was right, but that wasn't going to happen in the next ten minutes, so I darted up the flight of steps to relieve each man of one bag and hefted them as I followed Mary. They completed the look if nothing else, but goodness they were heavy – like, ridiculously heavy and were making my shoulders ache before I got to the bottom of the stairs.

'What on Earth have you got in here, Mary?'

'Gin,' she said pointing to the suitcase in my right hand. 'And tonic,' she pointed to the left. 'If you remember, they ran out of tonic once. You told me all about it and I thought I ought to come prepared.'

'Do you think you brought enough?' I asked jokingly, estimating that she could supply a bar for a week with what I was holding.

She puffed out her lips, not so convinced. Time was dwindling, so I picked up the cases again and got them to the elevator. We were already on the top deck, and the need to use the elevator had Lady Mary confused.

'Where am I staying, sweetie?' she asked.

'Um, the eighth deck,' I mumbled so she wouldn't hear.

She leaned her head forward. 'I'm sorry, could you say that again? It sounded like you said the eighth deck.'

The elevator chimed and the doors swished open. 'It is only temporary,' I assured her.

'But there's no sun down there,' she wailed. 'I'll have to come up ten decks just to find a bar.'

I plonked her suitcases down inside the elevator with an audible clink of glass on glass. 'Good thing you brought some supplies then.'

Lady Mary muttered under her breath all the way down in the elevator and all the way along the passageways, complaining that it was an awfully long way to walk just to find her accommodation. I chose to not point out that she was carrying only a handbag while I appeared to be dragging a hundred and fifty pounds of liquid behind me. I had to lean into it just to keep it moving.

I stopped at cabin 34662 which was as close to Mike's as Alistair was able to get. To the stewards, who were sweating profusely, I said, 'Thank you, chaps. We can handle it from here.' They departed with a quick nod of their heads to the passenger.

Lady Mary called, 'Wait a second,' while rummaging in her handbag. From her purse she withdrew two fifty-pound notes, handing one to each man. 'Jolly well done, chaps.' I was sure the stewards got tips all the time, but this was a surprisingly generous one.

'Is this it?' Lady Mary said, staring at the door. Her expression doing nothing to hide the horror she felt at slumming it. 'You know, Patricia, I wouldn't do this for anyone else.'

With a chuckle, I said, 'Thank you, Lady Mary. Your assistance may tip the balance in our favour.' The truth was that I had no idea how to employ Lady Mary but after my own failed attempt to get Verity drunk, I called in the heavy hitters. Or, at least, one heavy hitter. I had been in her company for twenty minutes and hadn't seen her imbibe any alcohol yet – a new record.

To answer her question, I said, 'No, Mary, this isn't your room. Your cabin is two doors along.'

Perplexed, her brow knitted, and she asked, 'So why have we stopped here?'

At precisely that moment, the door opened to reveal a rotund Hawaiian man with a big beaming grin. He whooped a laugh and rushed out to grab me. His arms wrapped around me, pinning my arms to my sides as he lifted me from the deck in a bearhug.

'Is that her?' I heard Rick ask from inside the cabin somewhere. Then he too appeared, shuffling from the cabin to greet me just as Akamu put me back down.

Rick was a little less gregarious than his friend, opting to shake my hand rather than crush my ribcage. Akamu in the meantime had identified there was a person with me and was moving to greet Lady Mary in the same full-on fashion.

Lady Mary danced back a pace. 'Touch me, savage, and I shall have you shot.'

Her threat stopped him dead in his tracks, Rick too swung his head to look at the small, but perfectly turned out lady offering to kill people by proxy. 'Is this her?' Rick asked.

'Who?' I asked, mystified for a moment. 'Oh, you mean is this the Godmother. No, this is my friend Lady Mary Bostihill-Swank. She's not used to being man-handled by large Hawaiian men. I suspect the same can be said for the rest of the British gentry.'

Under Lady Mary's withering gaze, Akamu backed away until he felt safe again, then his smile returned. Pleased to see me, he slapped me on the shoulder and walked me into his cabin just as the girls were appearing.

They weren't all staying in the same cabin, Alistair had arranged for them to have ones next to each other finding three in a row in close proximity to Mike's.

I air-kissed with Agnes and Mavis, then made a show of checking my clothing to see what they might have stolen from me. Mavis handed over my watch.

'One must practice or risk losing one's touch,' she said, which was as close to an apology as I was going to get.

Akamu, her other half, frowned at her. The guys, both former law enforcement officers, had chosen to turn a blind eye to the nefarious past of their girlfriends, but that was on the proviso that they would continue to behave. Since I knew Mavis and Agnes were only here because they made links in the criminal underworld and got themselves some fake passports, I had to wonder how often the subject became a fight.

Introductions were made, Lady Mary doing her socialite best and being warm to them while simultaneously trying to stay as far away as possible.

Once everyone had met, Rick pinned me down for some answers. 'So why are we here, Patricia? Your message said you were still dealing with repercussions from the problems in Tokyo. You said someone called the Godmother is after you? If it were anyone else, I'd have assumed it was a joke.'

'I wish it were,' I sighed. With the cabin door locked, the six of us were crammed into a tight space, but I took my time to explain about the gangsters in Miami, the Tokyo trouble, the Old City Firm in London, and how they were all connected by the Alliance of Families. I talked about the threatening letter, car chases and shoot outs, Jermaine getting shot, and how the Godmother herself was on board the ship so she could watch me wither and die.

Lady Mary screwed up her face at that point. 'If you know who she is, why doesn't the captain just arrest her and hand her over to the police? There must be a branch that deals with this sort of thing.'

It was Rick who answered. 'Because she's too well connected.'

I nodded sadly. 'She'll slip away at some point, either rescued by her people, or set free by cops on her payroll. The only way out is to beat her.'

'Beat her how?' asked Lady Mary.

There it was. The golden question. The one to which I still didn't have a good answer.

'I have a man with her now. You remember Lieutenant Schneider?' I got a round of nods and yesses. 'He's acting as their chauffeur to gather evidence if he can. We have also identified a number of her people on board the ship and two of them were killed earlier by my police-appointed bodyguard. At least, I expect to find they both work for her. They were both killed before anyone could question them.'

My skull itched again.

Akamu got back to his feet. 'So our job is to bolster your numbers and help you find something we can use to prove her guilt. We need something she cannot escape from because it implicates enough people for the law enforcement people on her payroll to back away.'

'Something like that, yes. Admission to murder would be good.' I thought about the recording I had on my phone and knew it wasn't enough to get a conviction. 'I have to head back up now. I'll be missed soon, and Verity could return at any time. There is a ceremony for Jermaine in less than an hour and she will be there with me. I'll have Lieutenant Baker and Mike Atwell, he's the detective sergeant I told you about, come here to find you shortly.' I gave them what I hoped was a confident, winning smile. 'Together, we can beat her. I just know it. She must still be running her criminal empire while she is on the ship with me. We just haven't worked out how. If we can figure that bit out, I'm sure we can get her.'

Lady Mary touched my arm. 'What do you want me to do, sweetie?'

I gave her a grin. 'Do what you do best.'

Commander Philips

My steps felt lighter on the way back up. All but one of the people I sent messages to were now on the ship. It was great to have a few numbers to back me up, especially since Verity didn't know about any of them, but it wasn't like we could win in a fight. Or maybe we could, but not without casualties on both sides, plus the possibility of innocents being harmed.

We were a long way from winning yet. A very long way, but I was being proactive, and the team were behind me. It was more than I felt I had the right to ask for. Now I just had to get back to the spa by scaling down the side of the ship – easy huh? – and then hope that my additional troops with their eyes and ears would be able to turn up something we could use.

Back on the top deck, I left the elevator and turned left to get back to the suite above the spa.

'Excuse me, Lieutenant.' The voice from behind stopped me in my tracks and I turned to find a man in uniform bearing down on me. He had Commander's insignia on his lapel and a stern look on his face. I didn't recognise him, which meant he was most likely relatively new to the ship.

Unsure how best to play this, I snapped myself smartly to attention and waved a crisp salute. 'Yes, sir?'

Coming closer, he stopped, an ugly sneer ruling his face. 'What on Earth was that?' he asked.

Now I could feel heat coming from my cheeks. 'What was what, sir?'

'That awful salute. Where did anyone teach you to salute like that?' I'd thought I'd done a pretty good job, but clearly my ability to mimic what I saw the crew do wasn't up to scratch. Before I could say anything in response, he began to circle me. 'What a slovenly mess you are. That uniform is a terrible fit, your shoes are in desperate need of some polish, and ... my goodness what is happening with your hair?'

A fresh voice sounded across the open space. 'Ah, Commander Philips. If I might beg a word, sir?' Lieutenant Baker was here to rescue me, and I breathed a sigh of relief when I saw not only him, but Bhukari, Pippin and Schneider. Schneider was none the worse for his time spent in Verity's company. I could just tell the Commander who I was, but I worried it might embarrass Alistair further down the line.

Commander Philips didn't look away from me when he replied. 'When I am done with this individual.' He said the word 'individual' like I was something unpleasant to be held at arm's length. 'I want your name and number. You are going on report, Lieutenant. I have only been on this ship for a few hours and what I have seen so far does not impress me.'

I really wasn't sure what to say so I was keeping quiet. The four Lieutenants arrived next to us, drawing the Commander's attention finally. Baker was making insistent eyes at the senior officer.

'This is Lieutenant Fisher, sir. She is a ... special case, sir.'

'Special?' he snapped. 'I don't see anything special. I see lazy and unkempt. The four of you are demonstrating an acceptable level of commitment to your appearance, but ...'

I stopped listening and thus missed what he said next because Schneider had moved around to stand in front of me. His wide back blocked the commander's view of me and let me slip away. I got to the first passage and ran down it, pounding along as fast as I could go.

By the time I heard the Commander's shout, I was at the suite's door and hammering on it for Victor to let me in.

I could hear Commander Philips getting angry because I'd slipped away. He was swearing oaths on the almighty that he would find me and make me wish I had never been born. I could only assume the others had elected to leg it, because I could only hear one set of feet coming after me.

We were near the front of the ship where the passageways followed the curvature of the ship. It meant that he was in the same passageway as me but would have to go a few more yards before he could see me. If the door didn't open in the next second, I was going to have to make a run for it or face up to him and confess who I was.

Feeling like I had a nanosecond left to make my decision, and with my heart thumping in my chest, I accepted that I wasn't getting into the suite and turned to go. To get myself moving, I shoved hard against the door, aiming to push myself off, but it opened as I did with all my weight against it, and I tumbled inside with a squeal of fright.

Thanking my lucky stars to have avoided Commander Philips, the moment I hit the deck, I kicked out with a foot to close the door again, whacking it from Victor's hand and sending it to slam shut with a bang. Then I lay on the carpet in the suite's lobby, panting slightly until the footsteps thundered by outside. Only then did I relax.

'Can we help you?' said a man with a broad Scottish accent.

Oh, bother!

Knowing I had messed up and outrun one problem just to create another, I rolled onto my side to find a bewildered family of five staring down at me. It was dad who had spoken, the three children were clustered around mum's legs, the youngest peeking around the side of her skirt with a confused face.

Doing my best to bounce onto my feet and look sprightly, I ran a bunch of lies through my head to see if I could come up with anything that might explain my presence in their cabin. 'Hi,' I greeted them with a big wave. 'I'm Lieutenant Fisher. I'm here to give the children an official welcome to the Aurelia. I'm the … I'm …' I had no idea where I was going with this. 'I'm the official children's entertainer. Sorry I'm a little late. As you could see by my entrance, I am having to rush to get around the whole ship to all the new boys and girls.'

What now, Patricia?

I briefly considered singing them a song but ditched that idea when I remembered I couldn't hold a tune for my life.

'Can you make balloon animals?' asked the little one, still peering around mum's leg.

'Nah,' said her brother. 'Can't you see she's not carrying any balloons?' He looked to be thirteen going on forty and had the attitude to match. 'Children's entertainer,' he tutted. 'Some holiday this is going to be.' The ungrateful brat slunk off to the terrace, opening the door to let the stiff Scottish air in.

'Right, well, I can see you are still unpacking. I just wanted to pop in to make myself known. You'll be seeing me about on the ship, no doubt. So long then.' I gave them a big cheesy grin and a double thumbs up. Sensing that I must look like a deranged version of the Fonz, I grabbed for the door handle, taking three attempts to snag it, finally got my hand on it and bolted.

As the door closed behind me and I breathed a sigh of relief, Commander Philips said, 'Got you.'

I said something quite unladylike and kicked the wall in frustration. I was done with pretending. One of my favourite outfits was in the suite I'd just left, I still had to work out how to get back to the spa without Agent Garrett seeing me, and if I didn't hurry up I was going to be late for Jermaine's memorial service.

Commander Philips was bearing down on me, a look of menacing glee in his eyes. I drew in a deep breath and prepared to give him both barrels. Serendipity chose that moment to intervene and it came in the form of my favourite member of the ship's crew.

'Lieutenant Fisher, there you are,' said Captain Alistair Huntley.

He was coming toward me from the opposite direction. Which meant he was coming toward Commander Philips and the two men could see each other.

Commander Philips snapped out a crisp salute, probably the best he had ever performed just to show me how it ought to be done. 'I found this officer loitering and looking slovenly, sir. When I attempted to reprimand her, she ran away. Can I assume that she is a regular embarrassment to the uniform?'

Alistair slowed to a stop and looked down at me. I gave him an embarrassed look which said oops and sorry all in one go. He looked troubled, as if the last thing he needed was me making yet more problems for him. I couldn't guess what he was going to say but when he put out his hand for me to take, I was shocked.

So was Commander Philips. 'Sir, I must protest. If you are in a relationship with this junior officer, it compromises your position as captain. I shall have to report this to Purple Star headquarters.'

Alistair shot me a smile. It was warm and loving and the twinkle in his eye made my legs turn to jelly every bit as much as hanging off the side of the ship had. Then he looked up at Commander Philips.

'Greg you come highly recommended. You will be a fine addition to the crew and indeed to the ship as the new head of Engineering. Commander Ochi will be glad to have you on board to relieve him, as will I. He's been rather stretched doing two jobs these last few weeks. I wouldn't rush to inform Purple Star HQ about me just yet though, you might want to ask around a bit first. I'll leave you to get on Commander Philips, I am sure you have much to do in the Engineering department.'

Commander Philips wasn't happy being kept in the dark. 'But, sir, I... Lieutenant Fisher must be suitably admonished, sir.'

With a tug of my arm, Alistair led me around to the other side of him so he was between me and the commander, then he smacked me on the bottom when I wasn't looking. 'Will that do?' he asked Commander Philips as my face turned red. 'If you feel more than that is required, I might need to take her elsewhere.'

My jaw dropped open. What was going on today? First Mike thought it entertaining to make jokes about my weight as I dangled from a rope. Now Alistair was making public references to giving me a spanking.

It worked though – Commander Philips wasn't sure which way to look. 'Don't let me keep you,' Alistair called over his shoulder as he placed a hand around the back of my neck and started to steer me along the passageway.

'Just you wait,' I hissed. 'There will be a penance for this.'

He dipped his head to whisper back at me, his voice a soft growl, 'Oh, I do hope so.'

Distractions and Divorce Lawyers

I t came as no surprise that Lieutenant Baker and the others had alerted the captain to my plight. That he found me just as Commander Philips had was blind luck, but we were now cutting it fine to get to the memorial service that Alistair was giving and I still needed to get to the spa. There was no way to go down a rope from the balcony, not without Alistair creating a ruse to get the family out of their suite and he didn't want to do that.

Instead, the plan was to create a diversion that would distract Agent Garrett and let me get back into the spa without him seeing.

It felt like a lot of effort just so I didn't have to tell the man what I suspected. Honestly, if my head didn't keep itching when I thought about him killing the second guard at the elevator earlier, I would probably just come clean and bring him into the group.

We took the stairs to get down one flight to the nineteenth deck where Alistair kissed me goodbye as he went to the chapel to get ready. Emerging onto the deck amid passengers beginning to return from a day in Glasgow, we could see Agent Garrett already, keeping vigil a few yards from the door to the spa. He wouldn't be able to see us, and most likely wasn't looking for trouble to appear, but I kept back just in case.

Then I spotted Rick and Akamu. The girls were nowhere in sight, but they both possessed a unique ability to blend in and not be seen. It was one of the things that kept them out of jail. The guys, though, they stuck out like two sore thumbs. They were loud, usually cracking jokes, and if their personalities weren't big enough, they were both large men to boot. I needed to warn them, or they would walk right by Wayne.

I nudged Lieutenant Bhukari. 'Deepa, can you grab the guys and bring them back this way?' If they kept going, Wayne would see them, but their presence also created an opportunity. The attractive guard from Pakistan followed where I was pointing, saw the guys, and went after them.

Getting them turned around, they spotted me and were both about to call out a greeting when Lieutenant Bhukari put her arms around their heads and her hands over their mouths. They got the message and came the rest of the way being quiet and unobtrusive.

'Heeey, Patty. Hey, guys,' whispered Akamu once he was close enough. 'We were just following one of the targets. That Mike guy knows his stuff,' I figured that had to be quite a compliment from one law enforcement officer to another. 'Don't worry though, the girls are still on him. They think he's following some kid.'

I pushed his report to one side, focusing on what I needed to happen now. 'Can you guys create a diversion?' I asked, knowing full well what the two reprobates would do. 'I need to get that man,' I carefully pointed out Agent Garrett, 'away from the spa door so I can get in.'

'You want him unconscious?' Rick asked.

'What? God, no. In fact, I only want him distracted for a few seconds. Just long enough for me to get inside. After that, I'll be coming back out again.'

'Riiight,' drawled Rick, wondering what I might be up to. He knew better than to ask though, so with a grin at his partner, the two men set about creating a diversion.

Just as they moved away, I hissed, 'We're on a tight schedule.'

Rick rolled his eyes. 'When aren't you, Patricia Fisher?'

Young Pippin had been quiet for some time but spoke up now. 'Wouldn't it be easier if I just ran up to Agent Garrett and told him I'd just seen Mrs Fisher around the corner and she looked like she was in trouble?' We all looked at him. 'He would run after me,' he explained, 'and then I would have to admit I'd misinterpreted what I'd seen. I'd look stupid but the distraction would be done.'

He was right. There were far easier ways than getting Rick and Akamu to do something. Lieutenant Schneider managed to lift his foot off the ground in the act of going after the two retired Hawaiian cops, when it was very suddenly too late.

'Fire!'

The shout came from our left and was sufficiently loud enough to get the attention of everyone in sight. True to the word of whoever chose to shout, there was indeed a fire.

Schneider started toward it, walking backward so he could speak to us. 'I guess that's our cue.'

I had to go the long way around, which I did, hurrying because Agent Garrett, looking at the smoke rising from a large potted plant, could turn his head the other way at any moment. Meanwhile, I got to watch the four lieutenants swing into action. They did a fine job of making the ship's crew look efficient and calm in a crisis. The fire was out in seconds, Schneider snagging a fire extinguisher from a safety point on his way past and deploying it at the base of the flames even as he continued walking toward it.

I got to the door, watching Agent Garrett the whole time, and reached out with my left hand to push the door inward. I should have been looking where I was going because instead of door, I got boob. A large woman with a shock of ginger hair had opened it and started to walk out in the time since I last glanced that way. Focussed on Agent Garrett, I didn't see her until I looked down to see what I had my hand on.

'Hey!' the lady snapped at me.

I snatched my hand back, saw Agent Garrett turning his head to see what the latest noise was all about and shoved my way past her. She all but filled the door frame, but I wasn't getting caught now, not after all that effort. I popped out the other side, stumbled and corrected myself, and when the woman was spinning around to accost me, I ran past Faye on reception and kept going.

I could hear the ginger-haired woman complaining to Faye as I barged through doors and away from her. I was in. Now all I had to do was get changed and head back out.

Would you believe that it was only at that point that I realised I had no clothes to change into? My outfit for the day was still in the suite above. I doubted it was still laid out on the bed, but whatever Victor had done with it, it wasn't here for me to put on now.

I wanted to bang my head against the wall. Instead, I closed my eyes and drew in a deep breath. I could message Deepa and get her to bring me an outfit. I dismissed option one because I simply didn't have time if I was going to make it to the memorial service with Verity. Option two was to steal someone else's clothes. I didn't like that idea either and it would most likely look strange to Agent Garrett when I came out wearing something that was not only not mine, but also, chances are, didn't fit very well.

I sighed and went with option three, shedding the uniform and balling it up into a heap. Someone would have to recover it later because I was going out and back to my suite wearing nothing but a towel.

Super. What are the chances that this will go to plan?

You could see where my bra had left lines on my shoulders. They wouldn't be there if I had been in the spa the whole time, but I really couldn't fix that with the time I had. I just had to pray Agent Garrett wouldn't notice.

Back in the spa's reception, the ginger-haired woman was still complaining, but when she glanced my way, she didn't seem to recognise me. I'm sure there's a line in there somewhere about looking different with my clothes on. Anyway, I padded outside in my bare feet leaving little footprints as I went.

Agent Garrett gave me a single raised eyebrow. 'Wardrobe malfunction?'

'Yes,' I sighed, pleased to be given a cue to lie through my teeth. 'A tray of drinks got spilled and my clothes caught the lot. They were rushed to the dry cleaners already.'

'Your shoes too?' he enquired, making it sound like he didn't believe me.

'They don't go with this towel,' I snapped indignantly. 'If you don't mind. It's a bit cool to be out in just a towel. I'd like to get back to my suite now if you please.'

Miraculously, I made it all the way back to the Windsor suite without finding myself naked at any point. Admittedly, I avoided the elevator for fear the doors would perform the clichéd trick of taking the towel with them. However, rounding the final turn to my suite, I found two men in suits waiting for me.

My heart beat a quick staccato but only until I got a proper look at them. They looked boring, which is a different thing from looking bored. Both were in their forties, sporting hairstyles at least a decade out of fashion and pot bellies that poked out from their open jackets. They saw me coming and knew who I was, the spark of recognition obvious. Watching me approach with morose expressions, they looked like they could suck the fun from a kids' party merely by walking past.

I didn't need to have seen them before to guess who they were. They were lawyers. More accurately, they were Charlie's divorce lawyers and they had tracked me here.

I felt Agent Garrett tense even though he was behind me. A rather wicked voice in my head wanted one of the lawyers to make a sudden move so my bodyguard might accidentally shoot them both. Alas, they waited patiently, calmly, and with boring intent until I got within conversation distance.

'Mrs Fisher,' one said with a boring voice. 'My name is Hobbs. This is my partner Renshaw.' I rudely swiped my doorcard to open the door and pushed by them to get inside. 'We are representatives of Warhurst and Clay Family Law.'

'That's nice,' I sneered as I went to my bedroom and shut them outside. The recent letter from Charlie's lawyers sat in a low drawer in my dresser. I read it twice when it arrived and elected to ignore it since. Had doing so prompted this invasion? It felt wrong to be rude to the men; they were just doing their jobs after all. I got that it wasn't personal for them. It still felt personal to me.

I dressed in a hurry, short on time now for Jermaine's memorial service and sent a message to Verity, letting her know I was on my way but running late. A touch of makeup, a change of earrings, and I went back to my bedroom door, pausing for a moment to take a breath and ready myself to run the gauntlet.

Hobbs and Renshaw were waiting outside, not exactly poised to pounce – these were not men of action – but positioned so that I would have to deal with them.

Agent Garrett asked, 'Would you like me to eject them, Mrs Fisher?'

I had no doubt he was capable should he choose to do so, but also felt certain they would sue him should he so much as touch the material of their suits. I shook my head. 'What brings you here, Gentlemen?' I asked, moving past them on my way to the suite's main door. 'You'll have to walk and talk, I'm afraid. I have a memorial service to attend and cannot dawdle.'

It was Hobbs who spoke again. 'We are here to assess your expenditure, Mrs Fisher. It would appear that, under threat of mutual division of assets, you are now attempting to spend all that you have and more. Therefore, it is necessary for us to assess just how unnecessarily extravagant your current lifestyle is so that it can be taken into account when the joint assets are divided.'

We were in the passageway outside my suite, heading toward the rear of the ship. In the tight confines, it was easy for me to turn my head and watch Hobbs' face as he delivered his news. There was no trace of emotion in his voice or on his features.

Almost unable to believe my ears, I sought to clarify. 'You believe I am spending money that ought to fall into my husband's hands when the divorce is finalised? And you are here to calculate how much my half of things must be reduced by to account for ... what was the term you used? Ah, yes, unnecessarily extravagant. Have I got that about right?'

Renshaw piped up for the first time. 'Mrs Fisher you cannot possibly expect to be able to justify staying in the best suite on board the world's finest cruise ship.

This attempt to defraud your husband from his rightful share of your assets will only result in spending money you may wish you had retained. The house in East Malling, the cars, and all other items are subject to division.'

I was nearing the chapel now and longing to lose the two men. 'Do as you wish, gentlemen. Assess away. Charlie will get not one penny from me.'

My response drew a grin that passed between the two men: I was funny to them. They probably knew I was yet to appoint a divorce lawyer of my own which made me a mouse facing down a pack of lions. I could see Verity ahead of me, waiting patiently, and wearing black at the mouth of the chapel. She was the shark I had to defeat first. After that, if I were still alive, I could worry about Charlie and his greedy, grasping need to get everything he possibly could. There was a part of me that wanted him to have it all just so I could prove it wouldn't make him happy. It wasn't going to happen though; I was determined he wouldn't get his hands on what had become mine through the generosity of the Maharaja of Zangrabar. I had an idea for how I might achieve that which I wanted, but I was yet to give the dilemma the focus it required.

Verity was squinting over my shoulder to the lawyers following me. 'Who are your new friends?' she asked.

'My husband's divorce lawyers,' I revealed with a sigh. Her eyes widened which might have meant anything from her thinking I would be long dead before the divorce could happen, to planning to kill them herself so they wouldn't interrupt her plans.

'Are they coming to the service with you?' she wanted to know.

'Are you?' I demanded, spinning around to address them, and doing nothing to hide the irritation I felt. My phone beeped in my handbag, getting ignored while I glared at Hobbs and Renshaw.

'It will be necessary to monitor your spending, Mrs Fisher,' replied Renshaw. 'My advice, given freely, is to return to Kent. However, if you choose to remain on board, we will need to be close enough to monitor your movements. We have already retained cabins, the cost of which will be considered as part of the funds you are denying your husband and this will be argued to be taken from your half of the estate.' Renshaw stared imperiously down his nose at me.

I chuckled at them. 'Good luck with that. Near me is generally the most dangerous place on the ship.' With that I spun on my heel and walked into the chapel.

In Memoriam

The lawyers chose to sit two rows back from me in the small chapel. Alistair was at the front along with the priest and the pews were filled with Jermaine's friends and colleagues. Agent Garrett positioned himself right at the back near the door, standing guard and keeping a watch for anything and everything as usual.

I was feeling emotional even though it was all fake and my general sense of well-being suffered through not having Jermaine at my side. Worse yet, Barbie wasn't around either and I didn't want Sam to come, so hadn't told him about it. I was all alone, sitting next to a murderous underworld crime boss and had two blood-sucking vultures behind me silently judging my life choices as if they had any right to do so.

This wasn't a funeral; the pretence was that Jermaine's body had already flown home. It was a simple service of memorial and I wasn't really listening when Father McIntyre began talking, I was thinking about what the Godmother might do next. If her plan were to leave me broken and alone, she was going to go after my friends. I had taken three chess pieces off the board with Jermaine, Molly, and Barbie. There were others left though. Having rekindled my romantic connection to Alistair, a target appeared on his back, but Verity knew Sam too.

My heart made a double thud in my chest that was so loud I glanced at Verity to see if she had heard it. My hand wanted to dive for my handbag to snatch out my phone. I got a message a few minutes ago – it could be anything – but I was willing to bet it was an update from someone, and Akamu said the girls were following one of Verity's people who was, in turn, following a kid.

I had to look at my phone! I had to. My handbag was on the floor and Verity was right next to me, her arm linked through mine in support because I was playing the role of the bereaved. Had I played the role for long enough? Was she here with me so that she had an unqualified alibi while someone I cherished was attacked?

I slipped my arm from Verity's, causing her to shoot me a curious look. Alistair was just a few feet away addressing the congregation, his words passing over my head unheard as I used my handbag to shield the screen of my phone.

The message was from Rick – a question: Do you know a kid with Downs?

I shot out of my seat, shocking everyone including Alistair who continued with his eulogy despite the interruption.

Verity frowned at me and hissed, 'What are you doing, Patricia? Sit down! Quick-ly.'

I shook my head, I had to go. I was going outside to phone Sam right now because I was sure Verity was about to have him killed. She reached up to grab my arm so she could pull me back to the pew. Everyone was looking my way, more so when I snatched my arm away and started dialling Sam's number.

To heck with waiting until I was outside the chapel. I was going to call him right this very second.

I didn't get the chance to do so because in the space between heartbeats, a flash illuminated the inside of the chapel with a light so searing I thought I might have gone blind or maybe even died. To accompany it was the roar of an explosion, concussing my ears with its thunderous boom. Had I gone deaf too? My phone got knocked from my hands and might have gone anywhere. Then again, it could be next to my hand and I would not be able to see it.

Screams of panic told me I was still able to hear, though I had to perform a quick mental check to make sure I wasn't the one screaming.

Unable to see, I was completely discombobulated, seemingly disconnected from my senses until, two seconds later, my vision began to return. I lurched, off-balance and confused, grabbing the rear of the pew in front to support myself. The chapel had filled with smoke - thick choking smoke, which was yet to affect me, for in my stunned condition I was yet to draw my next breath.

Unwittingly, I then did so, hacking instantly on air so dense it had to be artificially produced. The chapel had become a hellish environment too deadly to remain in. Yet unable to see my feet, I wasn't confident I could find my way out.

'Patricia!' Alistair's voice cut through the din of other people shouting. It was followed by the sound of him coughing horribly. 'Patricia!' he managed again. Disorientated, I couldn't tell which direction it was coming from, but I tried to focus on it.

There were tissues in my handbag I could use to cover my mouth, but I didn't know where my handbag was. By my feet somewhere, but I was as likely to trip over it as I was to find it. My eyes were starting to stream, the smoke invading them to irritate and sting. Steadying myself and demanding I think rationally, I orientated myself using the back of the pew in front. To my left and right were aisles that led to the front and the back of the chapel. I wanted the back because there I would find the doors and escape. I wanted to shout to Alistair but doing so required a deep breath which I dared not take.

How could I not though? Was he injured? The sudden thought spurred me to shout his name, 'Alistair!' I coughed instantly, barely able to get the word out. Then a hand was grabbing my arm. I stumbled, tripping over something that might have been my handbag, then found my feet again.

The lights above us did little other than illuminate the smoke, but when the hand tugged me to my left and toward the end of the pew, I saw a rough square of light: the doors. Figures were moving about; rough shapes in the darkness silhouetted in the square of light as people from the congregation escaped the chapel. The air was filled with the sound of people coughing and choking, or wailing fearfully, but I hadn't heard anyone in pain yet.

'Patricia!' Alistair's voice again, and it came from behind me at the front of the chapel. Who was holding my arm then? It was a strong hand with a man's grip and too big for a woman. I smacked at it anyway, fighting to get free so I could return to find Alistair. I might as well have been a fly trying to shove a Volvo out of the way with my head for all the impact I had. As I dug my heels in, the grip simply increased, dragging me along in the wake of whoever owned the arm.

'Aaaarrrrghhh!' I screamed, clawing at the hand in raw panic and rage.

The dragging let up, but only so the person holding me could yank me closer to them. Suddenly mere inches from his face, I could see it was Agent Garrett. 'Mrs Fisher, please desist,' he shouted between coughs before resuming to rush me from the chapel and all the terrible smoke.

Suddenly, we burst from the darkened interior of the chapel and into the light of the atrium outside. The deck was littered with bodies. Fortunately, none of them were dead, they had merely collapsed once they could escape the terrible smoke and its effects. I saw the lawyers, Hobbs and Renshaw. They looked stunned by what had happened, their cocky smirks banished by my prediction of danger coming true so swiftly. I locked eyes with Hobbs for a fleeting second, but then

Agent Garrett finally let go of my hand. Free from his grip, I immediately turned on my heel and ran back inside.

I heard him curse and come after me, but he needn't have bothered because Alistair appeared the very next second, stumbling through the smoke, tears streaming from his eyes and carrying Father McIntyre like a baby.

'I think he had a heart attack,' Alistair blurted, doing his best to gently place the priest on the deck. Agent Garrett ran to help him, sharing the load of the overweight man as yet more members of crew rushed to lend a hand.

Staring into the impenetrable smoke, I asked fearfully, 'Is everyone out?'

All around me, people were still coughing and choking, but the crew not already trying to help their captain rallied when someone chose to take charge. They were going back in, forming a crocodile by linking hands like schoolchildren on a trip to prevent any one of them from getting lost in the cloying smog.

More crew arrived, doors bursting open in the passageways leading to our location as security guards and more reacted to the sound of the explosion. That was what I heard: an explosion, but the kinetic energy and destruction one associates with such an event were absent. If a bomb went off, where was the fire which ought to accompany it? Where were the injuries? Looking around, I could see no sign of anyone who was sporting anything more than a makeup disaster where the smoke made tears track through their foundation.

There was another thing I didn't see: Verity. A snarl creased my face as I remembered her trying to stop me leaving. I was going to call Sam and warn him. Had she known? Had she worried I might deny her another of my friends and somehow activated the explosion herself? I wanted to run now, run to find anyone from my team and get the warning to Sam via them.

Seeing a better method, I started toward the nearest member of the security team. I didn't know the man's name, but he had a radio in his hand and that meant he could call Lieutenant Baker or any of the others.

Before I could get to him, paramedics ran between us as they rushed to give aid to Father McIntyre. Alistair himself was involved in the effort to revive the ailing priest, giving chest compressions while another provided mouth to mouth. The paramedics stepped in, taking over and the whole area was full of people doing things and shouting into their radios.

The smoke still spilling from the chapel doors suddenly gusted and swirled as the crocodile of people emerged again. They were carrying Verity like a roll of carpet. She was clutching something, her arms folded over it to stop it being lost. Rage filled me, diverting me from the lieutenant with the radio to rush at her instead. Blood rushed to my head, driving me to consider throttling her, but her head lolled in the arms of the two men carrying her, and I could see she was unconscious.

Was this her doing?

I would struggle to convince myself it might be anyone else, but as the rest of the brave crew stumbled from the chapel gasping for breath, they cried for assistance for the woman they found and how could I attack her now?

Reporting to his captain, a man said, 'It looks like she got trampled, sir.' The man was bent double and sucking in gulps of clean air. A memory of stumbling and stepping on something swam to the front of my mind. It wasn't my handbag I stepped on; it was Verity. Had I knocked her out when I trod on her?

None of that changed that Sam was in trouble. I couldn't stay here a moment longer, I had to warn him. The lieutenant had moved away, but I ran to him, not caring that he was already using his radio to talk to someone else, I grabbed his arm.

'I need you to get hold of Lieutenant Baker now!' I ripped his hand away from the radio where it was pinned to his lapel and whoever he had been talking to was now questioning what happened to the rest of his message.

The Lieutenant stared at me with an open mouth, momentarily stunned by the crazy woman attacking him.

'Do as she asks,' insisted Alistair in a commanding tone, cutting through any need for explanation or discussion.

The sound of a distant shot echoed through the ship, the noise at once unmistakable and mocking to my efforts.

I felt emotion well inside my chest, searing at my throat and robbing my ability to breathe. Agent Garrett, nearer to me than Alistair, took my shoulders as my consciousness swam. The lieutenant was on his radio, calling for Lieutenant Baker whose voice echoed back a few moments later.

'This is Baker. Secretary, secretary, secretary. Deck eighteen entertainment plaza near the starboard arcade.'

Queen Takes Knight

The coded message cut through my heart and left me foundering. It meant a passenger was dead. Combine that with the shot I just heard and the certain knowledge that one of the Godmother's agents was tailing Sam, and it was all I could do to not curl into a ball.

Agent Garrett fussed around me, pushing other people back. 'Give her air,' he insisted, and something gripped me, infusing me with an angry new energy which drove me from the deck.

I had to know.

Had Verity been awake I might had found something to club her with, or genuinely tried to throttle her, but I knew I couldn't do any of those things without overplaying my hand. Once she knew I suspected her, the game was over and the chance to catch her out would be gone. So all I could do now was pray.

Alistair was moving, leaving the desperate scene at the chapel once he'd deputised the senior crewmember there to take over in his stead. A dead passenger in public view trumped the disaster we'd just escaped.

'Mrs Fisher?' Agent Garrett sounded surprised that I was getting up. Ignoring him, I kicked off my shoes, knowing I could run better without them, and abandoned them, and my bodyguard too as I raced from one awful scene to another.

'Mrs Fisher!' yelled Hobbs the lawyer, thinking somehow that his voice would hold me, or even penetrate my conscious thoughts. I put my head down and ran.

Coming past Verity, who was surrounded by people and being attended to by yet another medic, I spotted the thing she had clasped to her chest: it was her journal. It made me curious about it when I was already wondering why it was so special to her, but I wasn't about to change course now.

I could hear Agent Garrett's thumping footsteps as he came after me, but I wasn't stopping. Not for anything. Not until I knew.

Alistair glanced behind to see who was following, his eyes registering shock. It might have been that I was following him at all, or it might have been the expression I wore which I imagined to be much the same as a person charging a machine gun nest in a battle with the express aim of killing everyone inside. My jaw ached already my teeth were clamped together so hard, but I didn't slow down, and as Alistair started to run, I went by him, my own pace as fast as I could make it in my haste to see who the latest victim was.

Along a passageway, running as fast as I could with two men in my wake. I burst through a final set of doors and my feet slowed themselves at the sight to my front.

I couldn't see the passenger on the deck, but I didn't need to, for I could see Paul and Melissa Chalk and that told me all I needed to know. The couple were clinging to each other for support, tears streaming down their faces as huge wracking sobs made their bodies spasm.

Alistair and Agent Garrett caught up to me, coming either side to take my arms because, apparently, I had stopped moving and was looking ready to faint. Next to Paul and Melissa were half a dozen white uniforms; Lieutenant Baker among them as was Pippin. Mercifully, my friends from Hawaii were absent so Agent Garrett didn't see them, but I questioned if I really cared anymore.

With Alistair holding my arm, I staggered forward on legs which felt numb, approaching the edge of the circle which then parted to reveal a covered form on the carpet. Shielded from public view by the press of people around him, I could see Sam's shoes and trousers poking out from beneath a jacket hastily used as a makeshift blanket to hide the damage beneath.

My bottom lip wobbled, and I went to pieces. Collapsing to the deck, I found myself spiralling into a deep pit of hopeless despair. That is, I was until I saw Sam sneeze.

Startled, and holding my breath because I was so desperate to believe it yet couldn't allow myself to, I heard Lieutenant Baker sneeze in the next second. His sounded fake though and had been performed to distract anyone who might have noticed from the fact that Sam wasn't hurt at all.

I knew that for certain in the next heartbeat because my assistant giggled at himself. Schneider carefully kicked the 'corpse', reminding him to play dead and stay dead and when I looked up at the tall Austrian, he checked around and gave me a careful wink.

Oh. My. God!

Pawn Takes Pawn

Now that I knew, I was able to concede how terrible I felt. I was still coughing, and my eyes stung terribly. Lieutenant Baker assured me that everyone else had been evacuated to the main sickbay already. The doctors were there along with a cohort of the ship's medics to treat the dozens of people affected.

They were being treated for smoke inhalation and getting their eyes irrigated to reduce the irritation and swelling. I didn't resist when Alistair insisted I go too.

It was an hour later in the sickbay when I finally got to hear the truth about the events leading up to Sam's 'death'. My handbag had been retrieved, and my phone found thanks to my four lieutenants. I accepted them gratefully, and let the medics treat me though I tried to make sure I was among the last to be seen.

The lawyers were there, suffering from the effects of the smoke like everyone else. When they had both been seen, they gathered their things, clutching their briefcases like they were the most precious things in the world, and approached me. They moved more cautiously now than they had, perhaps concerned I might explode like a bomb if they got too close.

I lifted my chin, acknowledging them and begging they say their piece in the same expression.

A glance passed between them before Renshaw spoke. 'We have all we need for our report, Mrs Fisher,' he announced.

I challenged his statement, 'I thought you planned to follow me around and monitor my spending for the next few days?' They were turning tail and running home, that's what I was witness to.

'Yes, well,' blustered Hobbs. 'I think we have seen all we need to see, Mrs Fisher.'

'We shall see you in England, Mrs Fisher,' added Renshaw, already beginning to move away.

I let them go, glad to see the back of them and turned my attention back to the people around me. Strangely, once he was treated, Agent Garrett chose to excuse himself, leaving me unguarded for the first time in days because he had a task to perform. He didn't tell me what it was, and I didn't ask. I genuinely didn't care because he was leaving me with the four lieutenants and that meant I could get some answers.

Agent Garrett thought me to be distraught and inconsolable and thus unlikely to venture anywhere by myself while he was off doing whatever it was that took precedence over my safety. Once away from Sam's 'body' which was taken to the morgue, his parents following behind, Agent Garrett made sure I would stay put for a while and left.

Once he was gone, I slapped Baker's arm as hard as I could. 'I almost had a heart attack!'

He shrugged an apology. 'Sorry, Mrs Fisher. I sent a message to your phone. Did you not get it?'

They knew about the event at the chapel, which once the smoke had cleared was traced to a flashbang. I didn't know what a flashbang was at the time but had since learned it to be a piece of military ordnance that creates light, smoke, and noise, though who might have set it off was still to be determined. What Lieutenant Baker and the others didn't know was that my phone had been lost in the ensuing confusion.

The story of Sam's murder went like this: Rick and Akamu left Mavis and Agnes tailing a man identified as being one of the Godmother's likely assassins. As they caught up to their girlfriends, they spotted two more people who appeared to be tailing the ladies. Their years as cops allowed them to spot the cues, but now we had retired cops tailing possible assassins tailing supposedly retired criminals who were in turn following a man they believed to also be an assassin. The assassin, Mavis and Agnes reported, was tailing Sam. Unfortunately, Sam hadn't been with me in London when I was last with Rick, Akamu, and the girls so they had no idea who he was or that he was connected to me.

They sent me the question: did I know a kid with Downs, and thinking back, I remembered that Rick said the girls were tailing someone who was following a kid. I thought nothing of it because I don't see Sam as a child. However, that's not how Rick meant it. Just like Billy the Kid was an adult despite the nickname, to Rick and Akamu in their seventies, anyone under the age of fifty is a kid. Regardless, I didn't get the message until it was far too late and then the attack in the chapel happened and I wasn't able to do anything about it.

Getting no answer from me, Rick sent one to Jermaine who immediately jumped on the problem, sending the lieutenants rushing to Sam's location. Between them, they spotted an opportunity, hastily communicating back and forth so they were watching rather than moving in.

'It became apparent that the man following Sam was hiding a rifle inside his coat – why else would he be wearing a knee-length wax jacket inside the ship?' asked Lieutenant Baker. 'He watched Sam go into an arcade and at that point chose to run up the stairs to the next deck where the entertainment mall stretches down from the top floor to deck eighteen.' I could visualise it in my head. Like the shopping and restaurant mall in the centre of the ship which plunged down several decks to provide light, the entertainment mall with the arcades, cinemas, and other attractions, was much the same only smaller.

'The girls couldn't have followed him up the stairs, surely? It would have given them away?' I questioned.

Lieutenant Baker confirmed I was right. 'It gave us a chance to separate the other two who were following the ladies. Just as the ladies carried on past the stairwell door the first man went through, the next two men started to move in on them. Schneider and I intercepted the Godmother's agents. Using text messaging, we sent the girls into a passageway where we were waiting. It took seconds to disarm the assassins, who were both carrying machine pistols, but then we still had the first guy to deal with.'

'We'd already sent Sam several messages, but he wasn't answering them,' Pippin told me. I remembered how often Sam forgot to charge his phone.

Lieutenant Bhukari picked up the story. 'We sent Anders into the arcade to speak with Sam, hoping he would be out of sight of any more of the Godmother's people who might be watching. We also assumed someone would be, and that, like Jermaine, there was a chance to kill Sam without killing him.'

While Lieutenant Pippin gave Sam instruction on what to do when he heard the shot, the other three closed in on the assassin. They had the drop on him and got him without a shot going off when he saw them come at him from three sides. Sam came out of the arcade on cue and Deepa fired a shot which narrowly missed him. Suspecting that there might be more of the Godmother's operatives around, they wanted it to be reported that Sam had been shot, so Sam fell to the deck and played dead.

Sam's parents were not in on the ruse, and neither was I, of course, so if there was anyone watching the aftermath, they would have seen a convincing 'act' from the three of us. Only once they were out of sight was it revealed to his parents that he was unharmed. According to Lieutenant Schneider, Melissa had used some swearwords he'd never heard before.

The ship was still moored on the Clyde in Glasgow and would be staying later than planned to deal with the latest problem. Sam's parents were getting off with his body, continuing to play the part of the recently bereaved and heading for home. Sam was hiding out in the morgue and would be snuck off on a stretcher later. I was sorry to see him go, but I knew it was for the best and that the Godmother thought him to be dead.

Not that Verity would care, but the one person who nearly did die, Father McIntyre, regained consciousness. He had been taken off the ship to a fully equipped hospital where, they told me, he was expected to make a full recovery. He would rejoin the ship later.

Now that the story of Sam's shooting was told, I turned my attention to Schneider. I had expected to hear about his day chauffeuring Verity around sooner than this but there hadn't been time so far. Had he seen anything? Was there a slim piece of evidence we could now pick at?

No.

'We went to Sauchiehall Street,' he replied glumly. 'I got the impression it wasn't the original plan, but they genuinely went shopping.'

I blew out a frustrated breath. 'Do you think she suspected anything and that's why she changed her plans?'

Lieutenant Schneider shrugged. 'Maybe. They barely spoke to each other at any point and when she did speak, he never answered with more than one word.'

Lying my head back onto the pillow, I pushed the latest disappointment to one side. 'I saw something,' I announced to the four people around my bed. 'We need to get the team together as soon as possible.'

Four faces frowned at me with curiosity. 'What did you see, Mrs Fisher?' asked Lieutenant Schneider.

I tilted my head to one side, uncertain now how to answer his question. 'I don't know,' I said, giving them an unhelpful answer that made them all glance at one another in confusion. 'Something.' I was rerunning the aftermath of the chapel flashbang in my head. 'We were all outside gasping for breath and coughing when Verity was carried out.' My statement didn't make sense to my friends gathered around my bed in sickbay; I hadn't provided any perspective. 'The Godmother was clutching her journal, but she was unconscious.'

Lieutenant Baker hitched an eyebrow. 'How does that work?'

'It doesn't,' I replied, shaking my head. Focussing my thoughts carefully, and trying to remember the details, I said, 'She wasn't coughing either and she didn't have the streaks of tears running down her face that everyone else had. I think she knew it was about to happen.' I was nodding to myself now and getting a familiar itching feeling at the back of my skull. 'I didn't see it, but I am willing to bet she had a gasmask in her handbag. She stayed inside the chapel and pretended to be injured. It gave her an ironclad alibi for the attack on Sam which we all know isn't true. But she was clutching her journal ...'

'You think it might be important?' Lieutenant Bhukari asked.

I skewed my lips to one side and huffed a frustrated breath out through my nose. 'She writes in it every night. That's what Mike and Jermaine said from watching the surveillance footage of her cabin. Like a religious act, she opens her journal and sits with it on her lap for an hour or more. We need to have another look at that footage, maybe see if the contents of the journal are ever displayed.' A different thought occurred to me. 'You arrested three of her people today. Did you get anything from them?'

The Woman in Charge

'Y ou are certain they will not talk?'

The Godmother let one corner of her mouth turn upwards in a grin. To the man standing before her, it made her look like a shark about to bite. 'They know what is good for them. If they are jailed, what can they be jailed for? Apart from Marcus, who shot that annoying Sam Chalk character, the other two will be charged for possession of firearms. Their cabins will be searched by the ship's security team and the rest of their equipment will be found. Those idiots in their splendid white uniforms might be incompetent, but even they will be able to pin a conviction. All three will go to jail where they will be well looked after. The alternative is to go against the Alliance of Families and that guarantees their death. None of them are foolish enough to believe there is a third alternative where they somehow get into a witness protection program and survive, living until retirement age in Florida.'

The man drew in a deep breath, believing what he had just heard but not feeling comforted by it. 'And what of the two who were killed this morning? That makes the loss five so far.'

The Godmother merely chuckled. 'What of it? They are not necessary. None of them are. You play one of the most important roles. The rest are just security, or backup. A redundancy system if you like so that they can be called on if necessary. Now, tell me. Does she suspect?'

He shook his head. 'I don't think so.'

'You don't think so?' Her grin returned, unnerving the man to the point that he began to feel sick.

Clearly, she expected him to be confident in his answers. 'No,' he stammered. 'Nothing I have seen suggests she has any idea who you are. She believes the God-mother might try to target her here on the ship, but she still acts as if Jermaine's death was an accident that occurred as part of the stalker's attempts to kill Shandy Berkowitz. The latest death though – Sam Chalk - that one is going to hit her hard but when she recovers enough to think straight, she will know it was you ... the Godmother, I mean.'

Verity Tuppence leaned back in her chair, getting comfortable. She wasn't in her cabin; basic security dictated that she had several safe places on the ship to meet with her agents should she need to. Walter did a lot of it because Verity wanted to watch Patricia Fisher. Patricia Fisher was an enigma and one who demanded personal attention. It had been years since Verity found someone who didn't die the moment she sent people to kill them. Yet Patricia Fisher had now survived multiple encounters with various experienced and very well-paid assassins. The news of her escape each time, most especially the shootout in a house, defied belief and it was for that reason that Verity chose to involve herself.

Partly that was due to a touch of embarrassment over the intended victim living on. It was an insult to the Alliance and Verity was now suffering dissenting voices among her immediate next tier. Her hold over the Alliance of Families was based more on her ability to steer it profitably than it was on fear of what she might do to anyone who chose to challenge her. For almost two decades, ever since her father's death, in fact, she had led the Alliance and they had grown in power, influence, and size. The net worth of the organisation was larger than many developed nations' GDP.

All these things were in her favour, but an annoying fly in the ointment, which ought not to make it onto anyone's radar, had become a talking point among her peers. Her personal involvement wasn't necessary, but in the end, she realised that she wanted to go. There was a thrill to the kill which she hadn't realised she missed.

'I think Mrs Fisher does suspect,' she accused the man. 'Why else would her housemaid suddenly vanish?'

'She joined the security team,' he attempted to defend himself. 'She's in California now.'

'So you claim,' Verity continued. 'But it smacks of a deliberate move to me. Then her perfect blonde gym instructor friend also vanishes. Whisked away by her boyfriend at a most convenient juncture, wouldn't you say?' The man gulped, unsure what a correct response might be. The Godmother was known for having people shot just for disappointing her and he was on the ship to feed her information. Now it looked as if he was failing. 'It will make no difference,' she drawled. 'I will have the blonde bimbo dealt with later. Her boyfriend too probably, just for good measure. I wanted Patricia to feel beaten and alone. She has no one back home to run to for solace, so it's just her boyfriend, the captain, to go. Then, once she is broken and at my feet, I will reveal myself and you can be the one to pull the trigger.'

'Me?' He felt cold all over. Killing a couple of men when he felt he had no choice was one thing. Pulling the trigger in cold blood ... would he ever sleep again?'

Verity smiled as she watched the man squirm. 'Yes, you. What did you expect? You sold your soul the moment you took my money. Did you really think you would escape unscathed?'

The man knew why she wanted him to pull the trigger. After that she would own him forever. She would probably film it and hang it over his head. The money had been enough to sway him. In truth, he'd accepted it willingly, but now, when he knew what it was going to cost him, it wasn't enough.

'What should I do now?' he asked.

Verity flicked her journal open. It was the time of the day when she needed to conduct transactions and check on the business operations around the globe. 'You should go back to doing what you have been doing. Keep her alive for me. You have been singularly brilliant at that thus far.'

'You didn't give me much choice,' he murmured.

Verity didn't bother to look up, the contents of her journal drawing her attention. 'No, I did not. Taking a bullet for her, was I suppose, more than I expected you to have to do. It is almost done now though. The end, as they say, is nigh.' He turned toward the door, desperate to escape her presence, but her voice stopped him. 'One last thing?'

'Yes?' he enquired with a gulp.

'Please close the door on your way out, Agent Garrett.'

The Journal

My eyes still stung, but hunger, a feeling that I needed to get a shower because the cloud of smoke had permeated my hair and skin, and the opportunity presented by Agent Garrett having not yet returned, got me off my bed in sickbay and heading for Mike's cabin on deck eight.

It didn't take us long to get there but longer than it might because we took a circumnavigating route, otherwise known as the long way, to minimise the chance of running into Agent Garrett.

The Lieutenants all made phone calls, getting all the people in the team rounded up and moving to meet us. Most of them were still carefully and casually keeping an eye on the people Mike and Jermaine had identified as her agents. That was abandoned in favour of a new plan.

My phone rang, Agent Garrett calling me to find out where I was since I was no longer in sick bay. I switched it to silent and put it back in my bag. He would keep calling, and come looking for me, but I needed some time away from him.

By the time we got to Mike's, the engines had started, and the giant ship was getting ready to leave Scotland behind. During the night, the Aurelia, floating palace that it is, would cruise into the Irish Sea and dock in Dublin. Our time to catch Verity was dwindling fast since she was due to leave in Southampton. I was too, or at least, that was the lie I told her. With Sam pretending to be dead, plus Jermaine, Barbie, and Molly gone, I believed she was either going to come for me next or complete my downfall and take out Alistair first. Either way, it felt like we were in the end game and a new strategy was required. We got lucky with Sam; it could have gone the other way if the team had not been so vigilant.

What new strategy though?

'Yeah,' said Rick, always the sceptic. 'What new strategy?'

Quite how we packed so many of us into the small cabin defied belief. It was like one of those challenges where they put forty-three people into a small car. A knock at the door promised to add another one. Some shuffling had to take place just to answer it but, as expected, Lady Mary was outside.

'Greetings, fellow co-conspirators,' she barged her way into the room with a loaded tray of drinks. Looking around, she said, 'Ah, thought so. Nobody else thought to bring refreshments.' The tray of drinks went onto the small desk next to Jermaine's laptop and I rolled my eyes when she then added a tiny bowl of olives, saying, 'I thought people might be hungry too.' Lady Mary stayed stick-thin by dint of not bothering to eat: all her calories came in liquid form.

'Are we all here now?' I asked, already certain we were: four lieutenants, Mike, Jermaine, Rick and Akamu, Mavis and Agnes, and now Lady Mary. Alistair was safely on the bridge Lieutenant Baker had already confirmed for me. I felt sure he would not get harmed by the Godmother up there. Sam and Barbie were off the ship and I still had one no-show which, to be fair, had always been a long shot.

A distant rumble, felt through the deck more than heard, signalled the propellers beginning to churn the water. The Aurelia was on its way again, but my question had drawn all eyes my way and I needed to say something.

Akamu put his hand up. I lifted my chin in a motion telling him to go ahead. 'I just want to open this meeting with a no farting rule.'

I felt my forehead crease in wonder.

'Alright, already,' moaned Rick. 'I said I was sorry.'

'He farted in the elevator earlier,' Mavis explained.

Rick's cheeks were colouring. 'I'm not apologising again. If I feel unwelcome pressure I will go outside.'

Under his breath Akamu muttered, 'Like that will make a difference.'

I could see Rick was about to launch into a fresh offensive, so I cut him off swiftly. 'We need to review the footage of Verity in her cabin.'

'I thought we'd given up on that,' queried Mike. 'We watched her for three days solid and saw nothing of interest.'

'We need to focus on her journal.' I'd found Jermaine in the cabin when we arrived so the footage was primed and ready to go. Before I asked him to press play, I explained the thoughts running through my head, the ones which were making my skull itch. 'She carries her journal everywhere, never letting it out of her sight. I am going to try something later just to see what happens when I do, but if it is of desperate importance to her, perhaps it is the thing we have been looking for all along.'

'The piece of evidence?' asked Mike, sounding unconvinced. 'You think she might have written something in it that will convict her?'

I shook my head. 'I don't know. That's why I hope that with lots of eyes, we might see something. Especially, please look for any frames where the journal is facing toward the camera. Jermaine will be able to zoom in and focus on what is written. Isn't that right?'

'Hopefully, madam,' Jermaine replied. 'How legible the text is may depend on light and shadow, how legible her handwriting is, and a number of other factors.'

Regardless of the odds against us, I pressed on and the footage started to roll.

Verity was sitting in her cabin in a small chair with the journal spread across her lap where she held it in her left hand. It was facing her and thus away from us. To her right, a laptop computer sat on a side table. With her right hand, she was clicking the mouse pad and then tapping a few keys. Like the journal, we couldn't see what was displayed on the laptop, but after watching for only a couple of minutes one thing became abundantly clear: she wasn't writing in her journal at all. She was using it in conjunction with the laptop.

Mike and Jermaine had been listening for her or Walter, who was sat in the other chair mesmerised by the television, to say something incriminating or for a visitor to drop by to discuss my impending death. If they had brandished a weapon or done anything to suggest they were not who they were pretending to be, we would have gained a small piece of evidence to take to a law enforcement agency. They were too savvy for that, but it meant that both Mike and Jermaine had missed the obvious clue. They saw it now though.

'She's not writing in her journal at all,' observed Jermaine, the disappointment at not seeing it before was ripe in his voice.

'Her hand is across to the right side of the laptop,' observed Deepa. Her comment made us all look at Jermaine's computer and the number buttons positioned there the same way they were on every computer. 'She's entering number sequences.'

In deathly silence we all watched, no one saying a word as we focussed our concentration on the small screen.

The knock at the door scared me clean out of my skin and it made Akamu, nearest the door, squeal in fright.

Rick thumped him on the arm. 'Godsdammit, man. Look at the size of you, and you squeal like a frightened mouse.'

'Caught me by surprise is all,' Akamu tried to shrug it off, but everyone was laughing at him until I shushed them.

In a hushed whisper, I pointed out, 'If we are all here, who is knocking at the door?'

No one knew the answer, but what no one said was that if it was the Godmother's agents and they someone knew far more than we hoped, they could roll a single grenade into the cabin and kill us all in one go.

Through tight lips, Mike asked, 'Who is it?' He tried to make it sound casual but failed.

A beat of silence followed, broken unexpectedly when a voice said, 'It's me!'

The unhelpful answer didn't matter because we all knew who it was, Akamu squeezing forward so Lieutenant Schneider could wrestle the door open.

'Sam, what are you doing here?' I gasped, while holding my head in disbelief when my assistant poked his head around the edge of the door.

He poked his bottom lip out in consternation, looking as if I were now suggesting he had done something wrong. 'I'm part of the team,' he pointed out. Akamu got the door shut again, just in time for Sam's perpetual smile to return. 'Mum and dad are not happy,' he admitted with a grin. 'Mum said she is going to string me up by my Buster Browns.'

Okay, he didn't say Buster Browns at all, but I prefer not to discuss male genitalia in public, or at all, if I can avoid it.

The how and why of his presence on the ship could be discussed later. Right now, we needed to talk about how we were going to get our hands on her journal. Pointing to the tatty, brown leather book on Verity's lap, I said, 'We have to get that book.'

'Easy,' said Agnes.

'Give us half an hour,' added Mavis, both ladies turning toward the door.

I stopped them by saying, 'We can't let her know we have it.'

They looked at each other. 'Okay,' said Mavis. 'That makes it a little trickier, but still quite doable. Give us an hour instead.' They both turned to go again.

'You can't just knock her out either,' I called, guessing what they might have planned.

Agnes threw her hands in the air. 'You are taking all of the fun out of this, Patricia.'

I pursed my lips. 'We have to get it, analyse it and get it back to her without her ever noticing it has gone. What about when she is asleep?' I asked. 'Could we give them knock out gas or something once they are asleep, get it and get it back before they know?'

Lieutenant Baker grimaced. 'The ventilation systems are all linked. Put knockout gas in one cabin and you gas half of that deck. Chances are it wouldn't work before it dissipated out.'

'She sleeps with it in her bed,' Jermaine admitted sadly. 'I should have realised its importance long ago.

I patted his shoulder. 'None of us worked it out, sweetie. Let's focus on fixing this.' What followed was a spit-balling session where we tried to come up with some way to get the journal from Verity without her noticing it happen. Forty minutes later I called a stop to it.

Mike scratched his chin. 'It's a pickle, Patricia, that's for sure.'

A pickle it was, but the more I thought about it, the more I convinced myself that the journal must hold some key to her empire, and through it we might access all that we needed to get her off my back.

My phone rang again; Agent Garrett was getting impatient, but I was going to make him wait. If we were coming to the end, it was necessary to tick one more thing from the list of things to do. First, I called for quiet and phoned Verity.

'Patricia?' she answered, sounding both surprised and unsure. 'Oh, my goodness, Patricia, are you all right? I heard about what happened to that handicapped boy you befriended.'

I wanted to point out that Sam wasn't handicapped, and that he at least still had his soul, however now was not the time. 'Nevermind me, Verity, are you all right? I wanted to stay with you when I saw you were injured outside the chapel. You were unconscious I think, but then I heard the shot and I had to go. By the time I came back you were gone, and they insisted I went to sickbay.'

'I'm fine,' she said with a sigh that sounded a little too satisfied to my ears. 'I fell over something when the bomb went off ... or whatever it was,' she corrected herself as if unsure. 'I think I banged my head because I woke up outside. The paramedics said I was lucky because I ended up under the pew and avoided almost all of the smoke.' It was a convenient lie that fitted her circumstances perfectly.

'Listen, Verity, I phoned because I was hoping I could call on your help again.'

'Of course. Anything.'

Good. That played her nicely into my hands. 'I'm too upset to cry, and too lonely to stay in my suite with just my boring bodyguard. Will you meet me for a drink? I'm afraid I might get a little wobbly again.'

'I'll see to it that you get back to your own bedroom safely,' she told me in a soothing voice.

The scene was set. 'I'll be in the upper deck bar in half an hour. Join me when you can.'

We said goodbye with her promising to meet me soon. Once the call was ended and I was certain she wasn't still listening, I let go a breath I wasn't aware I'd been holding.

'What is the plan, madam?' asked Jermaine, concern etched into his face.

I let go a deep shuddering breath and started to lay it out. I had wide eyes looking back at me as I doled out roles for different people to play. They were right to question my sanity – this plan was nuts. We were too short on time for me to come up with anything else, and I truly believed it stood a chance of working.

One thing was for sure, we were going to find out soon enough.

Bait the Shark

Back in my suite, I dealt with the inevitable complaints from Agent Garrett. He was, of course, unhappy that I ignored his calls and chose to return only when I was ready. I had my entourage of four security officers escort me back to my door though, intended as proof I had been with them the whole time, which I had.

I felt a twinge of regret that he was still on the outside of our secret gang. Yet again he showed his worth and loyalty at the chapel, going against the tide of people trying to escape as he ran from the back to get me and drag me to safety. That he dragged me over the top of Verity to do so ought to stand as proof that my suspicions about him had no rational foundation, but then something about the rescue at the chapel made my skull itch.

'I am going out again momentarily,' I let him know, petting Anna and Georgie on the carpet. The girls had enjoyed a mostly quiet day; certainly they had missed all the fun, but I needed them now. And they needed not only their evening meal but a decent walk too.

'We'll be leaving you now then, Mrs Fisher,' said Lieutenant Baker from the lobby. The four officers were loitering just inside the suite's main door, not wanting to come in because they had work to do – Sam needed to be found a place to stay where he wouldn't be seen - and they had someone to visit. The visit was to get us ready for the hopeful possibility that I could get hold of the journal. They were also running surveillance, looking out for Verity because I needed to time things for her journey up from her cabin.

I bade them a good evening, despite the certainty I would see them later, and fetched the dogs their dinner. Delicate pouches of fishy flakes specially catered for small dogs went into two bowls. Eighteen seconds later, the bowls went into the dishwasher and I called for them to follow me, 'Come along, ladies, I think it is time we took a walk.'

Agent Garrett was already waiting for us by the door to my suite, opening it once the dogs were securely attached to my right hand by a pair of leads. The girls scampered out and I took them right, heading away from the upper deck bar I told Verity to meet me at. We were not going there at all.

With the dachshunds leading the charge, we set off along the ship.

Verity's passage from her cabin to the top deck had a natural route, but it wasn't the one I wanted her to take. I wanted her to have to cross the mall, so the gang were corralling her by shutting down elevators – easy when you're a member of the security detail – or locking/blocking stairwells – easy when you're a devious former criminal or retired police officer.

I spotted her coming out of a stairwell exactly where I hoped she would just as I rode an escalator down from the deck above carrying the two dogs. The mall was filled with passengers excited to visit the bars and restaurants dotted about the ship, and the mall at Aurelia's heart was where the vast majority of them could be found. It made for a confusion of people – the perfect place to accidentally bump into someone unexpectedly.

And that's exactly what happened.

On an intercepting course to Verity, I almost walked right by them, but the sound of his voice drew my head and eyes around in question. What I saw was enough to freeze my heart.

'Alistair?' I breathed; my voice almost impossible to hear above the general murmur of happy people around me.

He hadn't noticed me until that point but his eyes widened suddenly as he took me in.

'Who's this?' asked the attractive brunette on his arm.

His face filled with panic. 'Um, Patricia, I ...'

'What?' I snapped. 'You thought I'd be tucked up in my room, crying into a bucket and swigging neat gin from the bottle?'

The brunette sniggered. 'Is this the one you were telling me about? Granny Pants?'

From the corner of my left eye, I spotted Verity standing stock still just a scant handful of yards away. She wasn't the only one watching the public display as couples, groups, and families all took a pause or glanced on their way by to see the evolving scene.

I cut my eyes at the brunette, shutting her up with a dangerous glare. 'Now? You choose to do this to me now?' I snarled at Alistair. He was wearing his full dress-uniform and looked as incredible as ever. I'd always believed people thought me lucky to be on his arm, but I doubted they ever expected it to end like this.

When he detached himself from the brunette's arm and stepped forward, I knew he was going to say something. Anyone watching could see he was going to attempt to explain it wasn't what it looked like, but when the palm of my right hand slapped his face, whatever words he might have been about say, died before they reached his lips.

The sound of the slap echoed across the mall, silencing hundreds of conversations and drawing yet more attention as those who were not already looking craned their necks to see what they were missing.

I spun around and hustled back toward the escalator, my pace fast enough to make Agent Garrett need to hurry. A sea of people parted before me, clearing my route, but with Agent Garrett behind me, I let a small smile play across my lips when I heard Verity call for me to slow down.

She had bought it. Hook, line, and sinker. The shark wasn't on the boat yet, but was being brought to the surface so slowly it was yet to notice the bait it had been fed.

There was nothing on my mind other than the next part of the plan. Timing my arrival with Verity's and Alistair's had taken a little coordination. I couldn't receive messages because Agent Garrett was right next to me, but two of my four lieutenants were positioned in the mall, communicating with Alistair and I knew where they were positioned. A glance had been all I needed to know whether I needed to speed up or slow down.

I didn't know the woman Alistair picked as his fake date, but she played her part well and I felt genuine pangs of jealousy to see her touching him. I was thinking all these things when I saw the two barmen from the cabaret bar we visited yesterday. They were coming down the escalator just as I was approaching it. They were out of uniform and chatting with two attractive women their age.

My mind ought to have been on everything else but seeing them made me think about the hypnotist case and my skull itched.

Eating with a Shark

I didn't slow down for Verity and urged the dachshunds to keep going, striding with purpose as I crossed the mall. I was acting the role of woman scorned with a side order of already-had-the-worst-week-in-history. Obviously, I couldn't see my own face, but by the way people were avoiding me, I guessed it said everything I wanted it to and more.

Just before the escalator that would take me up to the next deck, I hauled back on the dogs' leads and scooped them, still without breaking stride.

'Patricia,' called Verity, now starting to sound a little breathless. It pleased me that she had to hurry to catch up and that it made her uncomfortable. It was a tiny thing, but gratifying, nevertheless.

On the moving staircase I stopped, Agent Garrett grinding to a halt behind me just one step down which put our heads at about the same height. Verity continued to hurry after me, scooping her own dog, Rufus, I noted when I glanced. Puffing a little, she followed me onto the escalator but climbed it until she passed Agent Garrett and drew level with me.

'Patricia,' she panted. 'I don't know what to say.'

'How about that I had it coming?' I replied with a tinge of melancholy. 'I was punching above my weight and should have expected it.' I was looking ahead, focussed on nothing while I made it look like I was beating myself up. 'I'm not going to cry,' I snivelled. 'Not over a man. He's not worth it.'

The escalator spilled us onto deck nineteen, one deck below the top deck where earlier I told her I wanted to go. Knowing our destination, she'd sent her agents to the upper deck bar in advance. I knew this because Pippin and Bhukari were in there now. Verity would reorganise her people and send them to our new location, but we had a window where they would all be in the wrong place.

Switching venues was always part of the plan. So too sending Lieutenant Baker ahead of me to make arrangements. Waiting for me was a table that would work for my plan.

A few yards from the escalator, Verity was probably wondering why I hadn't looped around onto the next one and ridden it up to the top deck. I came to a halt, looking at the deck and moving my lips as if arguing with myself. As Verity came near, I placed the dogs on the deck and turned to her. 'I'm not sure what sort of company I will be tonight, Verity. Everything seems to have fallen apart on me in the last few days. When I came on board this ship, I had half a dozen friends with me and a relationship with Alistair ...' I let my voice tail off, then sniffed deeply and flicked my head back while wiping at my eyes. 'I'm not going to cry,' I snapped to myself.

Verity put a hand on my arm. 'You poor dear. You look so lost. There must be someone we can call upon to lend you comfort.'

I offered her a broken smile and shook my head. 'I'm all alone now. In two days, we arrive in Southampton, from there I will go home and lock myself away. That person I told you about ... the Godmother?'

Verity frowned at me, unsure what I might say next. 'Yes?'

'That's completely real. I know you laughed at me, but I think she is behind what happened to Jermaine and Sam. I think she might be behind other things that have happened too, like the two fake security guards Agent Garrett shot this morning. I think she sent them to get me.'

'You cannot be serious,' she replied, acting her role every bit as well as me. She wasn't going to be the first to blink and neither was I. Or, at least, I might be, but I wasn't ready yet.

I gave her a sad nod and began walking, Anna and Georgie trotting ahead of me. Verity quickly spilled Rufus onto the deck and came with me, her dog skipping along excitedly with mine. 'I came here to get away from the danger she presented to my friends, but somehow I was betrayed, and she followed me here.'

Verity, her eyes agog, looked about as if expecting to see someone. 'Do you know who she is?'

I let a hard sigh escape. 'I haven't a clue. I guess I don't even know that it is a woman. It's only the silly title that makes me think it must be. The thing is, I came here to keep my friends safe, to protect what was dear to me, but I lost it all anyway, and now ... I'm not sure if I care if she gets me anymore.'

Verity gasped at me. 'You really feel that low?'

I ducked the question, unsure I could answer it without smirking that she felt the need to ask. She thought she had me right where she wanted me. In response, I said, 'Let's get a gin and tonic. If I'm going to die soon, I don't want to miss out on my last few drinks and I'm sure the Godmother, whoever she is, would grant me this one last wish.'

The restaurant I had chosen earlier was Jinseon, a Korean barbeque place I'd never been in before. I gave Verity that as the excuse for going there now, making it appear to be a whim because it was right in front of us. It was almost full, but at the edge of the restaurant, where the tables met the edge of the mall, the maître d found us a table for two – just like I planned. Agent Garrett took himself to the bar where he found an empty barstool between a middle aged man in a crumpled suit and a woman of similar years but clearly with more coin in her bank if her outfit and jewellery were anything to go by.

I watched him ask a question, guessing he checked if the stool was taken, and then saw him settle onto it, the well-heeled, but older lady, calling for the barman, and turning her attention his way. I didn't dare smile, even though it was funny to w atch.

It was tight at our table with the three dogs. I had Georgie on my lap for a bit, until our drinks came – I ordered two gin and tonics each and didn't mess about with anyone fiddling the shot quantities this time. The lack of space was deliberate as it meant we couldn't put our handbags on the table; there just wasn't space. Verity couldn't have hers on her lap either. With the journal in it, the thing was too bulky, so it went on the floor. She placed it inboard though, away from the open edge of the plaza and that foiled my plan.

However, I wasn't beaten yet. It was always a possibility she would put it there. 'Here's to hitting rock bottom,' I toasted, raising my glass but downing the contents before she could get to hers. 'All the gin in the world won't bring Sam back, but it might help me forget him for a while.'

'Do you think that's a good idea?' Verity asked, sipping her own drink.

I lifted the second glass. 'I wasn't bothering to think.'

She hadn't noticed I was using my left hand and was letting herself be distracted by my words and my actions so didn't notice me palm the gravy bone I had hidden in my right sleeve. I dropped it into her handbag without needing to look and tipped my second glass back.

All three dogs went for the gravy bone as one, each of them determined to get the prize and quite willing to fight for it. Sausage dogs might look cute and be funny to watch, but I'd seen Anna draw blood many times and, like any dog, there was more fight in them than you might realise.

The kerfuffle beneath the table made Verity splutter her mouthful of drink, putting the glass down as fast as she could to find out what was happening. I was looking too and gave myself a mental pat on the back for a job well done. Georgie, the smallest of the three by far, was inside the handbag, nothing but her tail poking out and the contents were strewn across the floor, including Verity's journal which she lunged for.

It had fallen on my side of the table though, and I got to it first, picking it up and turning it over with nonchalant disinterest.

Verity dove across the table to snatch it from me, grabbing it with an outstretched hand only to find I had it clamped in a vicelike grip.

'Whatever are you doing?' I asked innocently.

'Give me that!' she snarled, trying to keep her voice low but still making enough noise for a dozen tables around us to turn our way.

I thrust it toward her, pushing her back and into her seat. 'Have it.' I let it go, pitching a glance at Agent Garret who was now on his feet and looking to see if he needed to come over. He was facing the wrong way to see the well-heeled lady lean across and drop something into his drink, but I saw it. 'I merely picked it up for you, Verity,' I complained. 'What is with you and that journal anyway? I see you take it everywhere but never see you write anything in it.' I hadn't planned to pick it up, but when it came to rest next to me, it felt natural to do so, and I wanted to see how she would react. Her surge of terrified anger only confirmed what I believed – the journal was important to her, and that made it important to me.

Trying to compose herself after her ridiculous outburst, she tried an apologetic look. 'I'm sorry,' she actually apologised to me. 'It's just very personal to me. My father left it to me when he died, and it contains some precious memories.'

I let the subject drop but got off my chair to deal with the rest of her handbag's contents. With her watching me over the side of the table – I could feel her eyes on me – I scooped her belongings back into the bag and handed it to her. 'You might want to put this the other side of you.' I suggested.

Georgie got the prize, but I would be rewarding both my dogs when I got the chance.

Verity placed the bag on the other side of the table, back on the deck but tucked in close to her chair. The journal, however, stayed on her lap, clutched with one arm as if it might float away without her anchoring it. I thought the plan to be scuppered now, but after a couple of minutes, when the waiter returned to take our food order, she placed the tatty, leather book back into her handbag.

I breathed a sigh of relief though it was far too soon to do so and when Verity wasn't looking, I scratched my left ear twice. I couldn't see the person who was supposed to be watching for the move, but I was sure they would see it, and get stage three started.

More drinks arrived, though I sipped mine now. I hadn't been making much conversation since the incident with the journal a few minutes ago but believed keeping to my own thoughts following such a sudden death this afternoon was probably normal. I made sure to look glum and spent time staring at my glass, waiting … almost daring the Godmother to find a topic of conversation to bring up. The pieces were almost in place and if my luck held, we would be able to make our move soon.

The chance came just after the waiter returned with our food. I had pressed Verity into letting me order the mixed barbecue starter for two which was a platter of spicy meats. It came coated in sticky sauce which was over our fingers in seconds.

We'd been in the restaurant for less than fifteen minutes which was how long it took her people, previously positioned in the upper deck bar, to get the message, pack up and pay, and get down to us. Their arrival caused Verity to glance their way. I knew it would, had banked on it, in fact, which was why Agnes chose that moment to swipe Verity's journal.

The two Irish women were experts in many criminal artforms, among which they boasted to be excellent pickpockets, and purse snatchers. If they wanted to take something without being noticed, they did it. It would have been easy to just steal the handbag, or steal the journal, but I wanted Verity to have no idea if that was at all possible. They were sitting at a table for two with Agnes's back mere inches from Verity's in the tight confines of the restaurant. Sitting at the outer ring where the restaurant ended and the plaza began, the Irish ladies now had the journal and a way to make it disappear. A man in his seventies was shuffling past the restaurant, seemingly paying no attention to the patrons. Drawing level with the table where Agnes and Mavis were sitting, the natural swing of his arm came back with his next step, and as it went forward, the journal was in it.

The journal was only visible for the briefest of moments when Mavis placed it in his palm like a sprinter passing a baton. His hand went up under the opposite armpit and fell back to his side with no sign that the book had ever been in it.

The four lieutenants were on hand to give chase and create confusion if Verity noticed anything, but she didn't, and the sticky sauce was all over her hands to make things awkward just in case she wanted to give chase herself. I glanced across to the bar again, slowly letting go of a breath without letting it show I had been holding it. Agent Garrett was there and had he seen Rick going by, he might have noticed him. Like the Irish ladies, Rick was in a disguise of sorts, but I had nothing to worry about – my ever vigilant bodyguard was suffering from the drug in his drink and was now cozied up with the well-heeled middle-aged woman. He hadn't seen a thing.

It was done. We had the journal. Now I had to keep the Godmother distracted long enough for the team waiting just around the corner to find out what was inside, copy it if necessary and put it back. Copying it, of course, could be done by taking pictures with a phone and need only take a few seconds. However, we finished our starters and there was still no sign of Rick or Akamu returning.

I had to focus my concentration to stop myself from looking about and it wasn't easy. The longer this went on, the more likely it was that she would look down to check her precious journal was still where she placed it.

What would I do if she saw it was missing? How long did I have left to play out the rest of this game for that matter? If her efforts to make me miserable and alone had achieved a result she felt content with, how soon would she decide it was time to kill me. I felt like I was within touching distance of the finish line, hoping with all my might that the journal might reveal something … anything, that would allow us to manoeuvre against her.

The waiter provided bowls filled with lemon and water and handtowels so we could clean our fingers. I splashed my fingers about, cleaning the sticky sauce away to distract myself from my rising fear.

How much longer were they going to take? My nerves were making me feel sick, not least because two pairs of the Godmother's agents were led to nearby tables. That they would be watching was inevitable and an added layer of risk I didn't want to take.

Neither Verity nor I had spoken since the incident with the journal and it was beginning to feel very unnatural. How long would she tolerate this now that she believed she had won?

I got my answer soon enough.

Through the passengers going by, I spotted Rick coming our way. He was heading back toward Mavis and Agnes, coming to return the journal so Agnes could slip it back into Verity's handbag.

It would be done in seconds, but fate chose to deal me a cruel blow. Just before Rick got to Mavis, Verity dabbed her mouth with a napkin and placed it on the table. 'If you'll excuse me. I must powder my nose.'

I had no reaction time! She was already pushing back her chair and reaching down with her right hand to collect her handbag.

Panicked into action, I blurted, 'Can't it wait? Our meals are coming.'

She stopped moving, staring at me for a few seconds. Her bottom was no longer in contact with her chair and from where I sat, it looked as if her hand was already on her handbag.

This Pork is Delicious!

R ick had stopped moving, seemingly frozen in time as he stared in horror at Verity. We were totally busted!

I couldn't breathe. We had come so close.

'Your entrées,' announced the waiter, sashaying back to our table with several plates balanced on his left arm and another held in his right.

Verity stared right into my eyes, assessing me, and saying nothing as another beat passed. She had seen something or recognised something in the way I acted when she moved to stand up. Inadvertently, my actions or mannerisms had tipped her off and now she knew that I knew.

When she sat down and moved her napkin to make space for the waiter to put the plates down, it surprised me. Shocked me right to my core might be a more accurate description. We continued to stare at one another, neither blinking while the waiter arranged the plates and cutlery, announcing each dish with unnecessary panache. With a small bow he departed, probably sighing at his wasted effort for the two women never once looked his way.

Finally, and with great effort, Verity tore her eyes from mine, looking down at the food and then back up at me with a smile. I was a guppy being stared at by a shark and the shark knew it could choose to eat the guppy at its leisure. Unable to feel my legs, and terrified I might wet myself in terror, I turned my head slightly to look at a table just across from us.

A man and a woman, both in their thirties and wearing the kind of clothes one might choose for action rather than fashion, looked directly at me, their expressions intense. When I gulped, they swung their eyes a few degrees to look at Verity. The Godmother gave a very small shake of her head and said, 'Not tonight. I think.' Then she looked at me, her expression victorious. 'Well, this all looks delicious. Eat well, Patricia. One never knows which meal might be one's last.' With a sly grin, she forked a piece of pork into her mouth - all pretence that she was my good friend here to support me was gone.

I could feel a need to swallow but couldn't work out how to connect my brain to the muscles that would make that work. Her assassins had just asked her if they should shoot me. If she had nodded the affirmative instead of shaking her head, I think it would have happened instantly and in full view of everyone. Furthermore, I suspect Verity would have continued eating her evening meal, delicately dabbing away dobs of sauce from her lips until ship security arrived.

Behind her, Rick passed the journal back to Mavis and briskly walked away again.

'You really should eat some of this, Patricia,' chided Verity with a frown. Then, seeing my rigid face, she put down her knife and reached forward with her right hand to put it on top of mine. 'It's all right, Patricia,' she soothed. 'You were never going to win. If it's any consolation, you didn't stand a chance, but you did play the game well. For the longest time, I thought you suspected nothing and that disappointed me, I don't mind saying. After the mess you made in Miami, Tokyo, and London, and then evading my assassins, I expected to come up against a formidable opponent, so imagine how I felt when you appeared to be walking meekly into my trap.'

I gulped, unable to form a response.

'Ooh, this pork is to die for.' She made her eyes twinkle. 'Get it? To die for?' She chuckled to herself but then sighed because I was proving to be a tough audience for her humour. 'Anyway, it pleases me to see that you really were trying to work things out. I began to suspect when your blonde friend took off. She only had a few hours to live, but don't worry, I will catch up to her soon. You could save me some bother and tell me where she is ...'

She waited for me to answer.

'No? That is disappointing,' she sighed again. 'I assume the fight with your dashing captain earlier was for my benefit too. Well done, by the way, it was very convincing. I think, had you not tried to get hold of my journal, I might have never known you were on to me. What was it?' she enquired, an engaging smile on her face, she was so keen to hear what I had to reveal. 'Go on, Patricia, you can tell me,' she encouraged.

Finally finding my voice, I managed to croak, 'Rufus.' Verity tilted her head to one side in question. 'His name isn't Rufus.'

Now Verity frowned. 'How can you know that?'

I reached forward to my glass with a shaking right hand, sipping the drink because my mouth felt so dry. 'He has a tag on his collar,' I explained. 'It displays a different name, and he responds to it.'

She nodded her head in a rueful manner. 'That horrible little mutt. I thought it would be a clever way to get to know you. An icebreaker if you will, but he's far more trouble than he is worth. I shall probably pitch him overboard later.'

'Where did you get him?' I asked.

Surprised by my question, Verity choked out a snort of laughter. 'The dog? You are going to die shortly, sooner rather than later if you continue to refuse to eat with me,' she snapped, 'and you are worried about the dog. I took him from the railing outside the post office in Longwell Green. Does that answer satisfy you?'

'Yes, thank you,' I replied, picking up my fork and spiking a piece of the pork. She was right about the taste: it was delectable. 'What happens now?' I asked.

Verity continued to chew her mouthful, stabbing another piece of pork, and holding it in front of her face as if to inspect it. I thought perhaps she was not going to answer, but she did. 'We arrive in Dublin in the next few hours and I have decided I would like to explore the city. Funnily enough, I have never been. Running an empire takes up so much time.' She was actually complaining to me. 'I call it an empire because it is the largest the world has ever known. Far greater than the British Empire, mine operates in every nation on the planet. My father started it all, but I am the one who unified the families, brought them up to date and created a singular management system.' She looked down at her piece of pork again, studying it critically. 'I will summon you tomorrow when I feel it convenient. It will happen on board the ship, so don't do anything silly like attempting to flee to a new destination. If you leave the ship, or if you do not come promptly when you are summoned, I will kill those four lieutenants you have working for you. I will kill your bodyguard Agent Garrett, and I will most certainly kill Captain Alistair Huntley. After that, I will still kill you. I may or may not go after your blonde friend. I think I shall, but your sensible cooperation may aid me to change my mind. Do not attempt to alert any of these people or my list of victims will simply grow. Is that understood and simple enough?'

The woman was asking me about giving my life up as forfeit as casually as if I had lost a hand of cards and had to buy the next round of drinks as a penalty. Her eyes flicked from her fork to stare directly at me as she waited impatiently for my answer.

I nodded my head.

'I need to hear you say it,' she insisted. 'Say you understand that when summoned you will surrender yourself.'

Swallowing hard and fighting a growing wave of nausea, I stuttered, 'I understand.'

'Jolly good.' Verity popped the piece of pork in her mouth, put the fork back on the table, and stood up. 'Enjoy the rest of your evening, Patricia. I will see you tomorrow.' In a swift motion, she reached down for her handbag, plucking it from the floor and slipping it into the crook of her right arm. One corner of the journal poked from the top.

Without a further word, or a glance in my direction, she left the restaurant, several tables emptying as she passed them – her agents abandoning any pretence they were here for dinner.

I was shaking uncontrollably by the time she was out of sight, adrenalin washing from my bloodstream to leave me feeling utterly exhausted

Mavis twisted her torso around until she was facing me. 'She's fun,' she laughed. 'Shall we see what they found in that book?'

Code Breakers

W hen I didn't get up and didn't speak, Agnes got out of her seat and came to sit in Verity's. 'Are you all right, Patricia?' she asked.

I nodded even though to do so was a lie. 'I'll be fine,' I replied, which was slightly closer to the truth but still a little hopeful. 'I'm just a little rattled. It's not often someone invites me to my own execution and insists I turn up for it.'

Lady Mary appeared at my side. Snagging a chair from a table formerly occupied by the Godmother's agents, she dropped into it and handed me a fresh glass of gin and tonic. 'Have that, sweetie, it will calm your nerves.'

I doubted it would do any such thing, but I drank it anyway.

While I tried to focus on the delicate, yet heady mix of botanicals, Mike Atwell arrived. He had Agent Garrett with him but was holding him up, Wayne's arm pulled over Mike's shoulder and held there to keep him upright.

'I might have overdone it on the rohypnol,' admitted Lady Mary. It was her assigned task to drug the poor man. Just like I felt bad about keeping him the dark, I felt worse about the need to drug him, but he would never have agreed to let me go without him this evening, and he would have recognised Rick or Akamu, or maybe even Mavis and Agnes even though they were all wearing disguises. Additionally, I wasn't sure how things would go with the Godmother when we tried to swipe her journal and could not have him intervening. So now he was drugged and would sleep the rest of the evening in a blissful state of unawareness.

Agnes frowned. 'How many did you give him?'

Lady Mary said, 'All of them. How many should I have used?'

Agent Garrett's eyes were so dilated they were all but entirely black and seeing them triggered a memory. It made me laugh, a chuckle bursting from my lips to astonish my friends. In all the insanity around me, I believed I had just solved the hypnotist robberies.

I drew in a deep breath, downed the rest of the gin Lady Mary brought me and got to my feet in a surge of motion. It was time to go. 'Anna. Georgie. Come on, girls,' I called, but when I looked, there were three dachshunds looking up at me.

'She forgot her dog,' said Lady Mary.

'No,' I shook my head. 'It's not her dog.' Remembering her threat to toss Rufus overboard, I smiled down at him. 'Hello again, Smoky.' I was going to call him by his real name and if I got a chance, I was going to deliver him back to his owner in England.

We decamped to a new location - a briefing room on deck seventeen. This was largely because we just didn't fit in Mike's tiny cabin anymore, but mostly because the briefing room gave us a base of operations and that was what this was about to become: an operation.

It all hinged on the journal giving us something we could use, because if it didn't, I was left with showing up to my own execution tomorrow. Baker and Schneider took it on themselves to drop Agent Garrett back in my suite. He would be out for many hours and that gave us time to come up with something.

Lieutenant Bhukari was waiting for us at the door to the briefing room, checking up and down the passageway before swiping the door lock with her security team card.

Coming through the door, my heart welled at the people I could see waiting for me inside. Sam was there, so too Alistair, who came over to wrap me into a hug.

Pressing my face against his chest, I heard him say, 'You, my dear lady, have a mean right hook.' The rumble of his voice came through his chest as much as I heard it from his mouth. It was a comforting sensation I yearned to feel again soon when this was over.

We parted, both wanting more but knowing this was neither the time nor the place for it. Rick, and Akamu were with me, so too the Irish ladies, Agnes and Mavis, all four had accompanied me up from the restaurant. Mike and Lady Mary moved around the room, making space by the door rather than hover there. Agent Garrett would be deposited back in his bedroom in my suite to release Lieutenants Baker and Schneider. It was a team, but if I included Alistair, there were only five persons with weapons, and it wasn't fair to ask anyone else to take up arms against the trained assassins Verity had at her disposal.

Five armed cruise ship crew members against an unknown number of heavily armed assassins. It wasn't enough, but how could we add to it when we could not tell who on the crew might have been bought or coerced. Some had, that was for certain, so if Alistair were to mount a force to take the Godmother down, he risked tipping her off the moment he started.

She held all the cards still so it came down to a simple equation: we found a way to force her to back off, or we would lose.

'Patty!' exclaimed Barbie,' bouncing to her feet to greet me. When I came through the door, she was sitting at a long desk that dominated the centre of the room. There had to be half a dozen laptops, all networked together with cables running all over the table like an upended bag of snakes. When Hideki and I faked her leaving the ship this morning, they drove around in a big loop to arrive back on quayside less than thirty minutes later. By then, he had explained some of the plan he and I had concocted, and they were both wearing different clothes just in case Verity had people watching. Verity could send people to track my blonde friend down, but they would need to look under their noses to find her.

We embraced and air-kissed, Hideki nodding his head at me in greeting.

'What have we got?' I asked, trepidation on my breath.

Barbie took my hand to tug me toward the table. 'Nothing yet,' she replied, somehow not sounding too disappointed about it.

'It's not a journal, madam,' Jermaine supplied, which set my mind at ease a tiny amount.

Inevitably, I asked, 'What is it then?'

My butler pushed against the table, rolling his chair back a yard so I could see the screen his body hid. 'It's a code book, madam.' I was looking at photographs taken of the pages inside Verity's journal. It looked like nothing but gibberish to my eyes.

'Do we need to break it?' I enquired, probably showing how little I knew about such things.

Barbie said, 'Sort of.' Her statement did nothing to help me but seeing my perplexed expression, she sat back in her chair. 'There are a hundred and twenty-two pages in total and each page has thirty-six lines. Not every page is full, and of those that are, some contain random annotations. We are focussing on the alphanumerical sequences contained within the book in the hope that we can develop them into a language of some form.'

She might as well have delivered her explanation in Klingon.

Seeing my continuing confusion, Barbie patted my arm. 'Don't worry, Patty, we have software to assist us.' She wasn't the only one working on the problem. It was kept within the established team, so Deepa, Pippin, Hideki, Jermaine, Barbie, and when he returned, Lieutenant Baker were all at a laptop. They were sharing information, eliminating possibilities, and working toward a solution.

Nothing was happening though and watching them was driving me a little frantic.

'I say, sweetie,' said Lady Mary, sidling up next to me. 'I don't see any refreshments,' she made a point of looking around the briefing room. 'Do you think we should order something in before people all begin to die of thirst?'

I'd had enough gin, a concept lost on my socialite friend. 'I'm sorry, Mary ...' I was about to say that we were in a lock-in situation, but before I could complete the sentence, it occurred to me that Verity was probably good to her word. She wasn't going to kill me until tomorrow so I could do what I wanted tonight. What I couldn't do was stay in the briefing room, biting my nails and fretting while my wonderful friends tried to break the Godmother's code.

Lady Mary was watching my lips, waiting for me to finish my sentence. Thinking the pause might have gone on long enough she prompted me to continue, 'I'm sorry, Mary ...' she made a spooling motion with her right hand, urging me to complete what I had been saying.

A grin spread across my face. 'Anyone fancy going to a cabaret act?'

... and You're Back in the Room

My suggestion was met with incredulous looks. Had Patricia lost her mind? To me, it felt completely sane to go because I was going to drive myself nuts staying in the briefing room. If Barbie and the others broke the code, they would let us know and we would abandon the cabaret bar. Until then, the less technologically savvy among us were just spinning our wheels and achieving nothing.

I wasn't dressed for a night out, and neither was anyone else, except Alistair, in his dashing white uniform, and Lady Mary, who claimed she didn't care where we went so long as they had a bar. That was a good thing because I had a plan for h
er.

The cabaret bar was one of the smallest on the ship, I judged, which Alistair confirmed when I asked him. The acts Purple Star Cruise Lines provided to the ship came without any agreement or say so on his part. Entertainment was managed by a completely different division of the cruise line at their headquarters in California and by an entertainment manager on board. Lieutenant Commander Krill, as Alistair explained it, held an honorary rank and was expected to wear uniform only on formal occasions. He managed the ship's stage productions and cabaret acts, the hiring and firing, should such a thing be necessary, and Alistair made it sound like he was relieved to not have the task on his plate.

It sounded like an easy life to me: they performed twice a day, an early evening and mid evening performance, but it wasn't every day because they wouldn't perform if the ship were in dock. I had no idea what they got paid, but I expected they got their accommodation thrown in for free and they always had new people to draw in because the passengers on the ship changed continually.

Seven of us walked through the doors … sorry, it's probably a mystic portal having met Will Controller and listened to his claptrap earlier. We had to leave Sam behind, much to his dismay. I genuinely believed there was a high likelihood the Godmother had withdrawn all her troops, but the chance that he might be spotted was too high. What would Verity do if she learned he was still alive? I didn't want to give it much thought.

On the way up from the briefing room, I chose to let go Alistair's arm to have a quiet chat with Lady Mary. If I was right, and my itchy skull told me I was, then she would be the perfect bait for the trap but she couldn't do the job alone. Surrounded by my friends and with Alistair by my side, I felt almost relaxed. Certainly, the stomach-churning terror I felt over dinner with Verity had passed. Alistair took the precaution of posting six security guards at the bar's entrance just in case the Godmother should feel it necessary to go against her word, and also because I'd told him my theory and he believed he would soon need them to perform an arrest.

Inside the cabaret theatre, we spread out, acting as though we were not together. Once again, without my friends around, I began to feel nervous, but when the champagne hit my system, I managed to shrug off my worries and focus on the sh ow.

Will Controller's assistant flounced onto the stage wearing a sparkly bikini. It was different from the one she wore earlier but contained no more material. It was little more than a spider's web with some crystals glued to it. She introduced the act in a fake posh voice, stepping back with a swish of her arms as a blinding flash and puff of smoke on the stage feebly attempted to mask Will the hypnotist as he stepped onto the stage.

The room was set out with lots of round tables facing the stage. Most were set out for two people, but some were larger to seat four. At each, the chairs were arranged to face the stage, leaving half of the table bare. The arrangement provided an uninterrupted view of the stage. Along the righthand wall of the room as one viewed the stage, the long bar was once again attended by the two barmen. When I saw them on the escalator, they had to have been on their way back down to their cabins to get changed because they were back in their uniforms now and the early evening act had been and gone while I was having dinner with Verity.

Lady Mary was the lone figure at the bar, sitting on a barstool with her legs folded at the thigh and flashing her devilish smile as she no doubt regaled them with anecdotes.

I could see the men smiling her way and chuckling, but their mirth was genuine rather than polite and faked. They were busy still, dealing with drinks orders brought to them by a team of three waitresses hustling around the room as they went back and forth with trays.

After several minutes of preamble, in which Will Controller explained the dark art of hypnotism to a backing track of mystical music, he got to the part of the show where he asked for volunteers. I checked over my shoulder at that point, worried Mike wasn't going to make it back. To play his part he needed to be better dressed than he was; the policeman's crumpled cheap suit didn't cut it if he was going to act as Lady Mary's husband. Thankfully, he wasn't much different in height, size, and shape to Alistair so we sent Jermaine with him to the captain's quarters to make some ... shall we say, wardrobe adjustments.

Mike came back through the door just when I was looking that way. One couple had already put their hands up – the ringers, Liam and Brenda. Will was making encouraging noises to get more people from the audience to join in, and Tammy-Jo was going around the tables, flashing her eyes (and boobs) at different men to get them on their feet.

Mike joined Lady Mary at the bar, air-kissing her cheek as a husband might and making sure to flash the Rolex Alistair hastily misappropriated from the fine jewellery shop on deck eighteen with a single call to the store owner. It would go back later but was another item of bait as we sought to determine if I had things figured out or not.

Lady Mary passed Mike a glass of what looked like champagne and then played out a planned discussion where he was trying to get her to join in and she was trying to refuse. It was loud enough that most people in the room could hear them, but it was a funny skit to watch. He grabbed her hand and tried to pull her from the barstool, urging her to get outside her comfort zone and mimicking Will Controller's spooky/mystical voice as he asked, 'What are you afraid of?'

When Tammy-Jo arrived in her sparkly underwear, Lady Mary finally relented, letting her 'husband' guide her to the front of the room and onto the stage.

At the last second and on a complete whim, I jumped to my feet. There were two chairs left and I wanted to see what being hypnotised was like.

'Patricia?' asked Alistair in question. I didn't ask him to join me. The captain of the ship clucking like a chicken could not be allowed, but that wasn't going to stop me.

Tammy-Jo was guiding a dumbstruck potbellied man in his fifties toward the stage on the other side of the room, and as I started forward, I spotted another woman getting up. She was here with a friend and had been trying to convince her to take part for the last two minutes. Tammy-Jo was going to get there first with her 'volunteer' which meant there was only one chair left for me and the other woman.

I hitched up my skirt and started running. She saw me, glanced at the stage, and started hot footing it too. It was a foot race, Will Controller spotted us and commented that his hypnotic effect was already working since his subliminal messages were drawing people to the stage.

It was a load of guff, but the younger woman had been sitting closer to the stage and was going to get there first. Seeing that I would lose, I grumbled something unprintable in my head, but suddenly the poor girl tripped. Too busy watching me, she found a drink spill or an obstacle with her leading foot and went down with a girlish squeal.

Two more strides carried me to the short flight of steps to get me onto the raised stage and victory was mine as I plopped into the last chair. I got a raised eyebrow from Mike, who was wondering what I was playing at no doubt; this wasn't the plan as discussed.

Straightening the creases out of my dress, I looked down at the poor woman who was getting a hand up and I saw what tripped her – it had been Rick's outstretched foot. He and Akamu were picking her up from beside the table of four where they sat with Agnes and Mavis. I guess they had seen me, and Rick chose to intervene in my favour as the poor woman passed them.

Ignoring her plight, Will Controller pressed on with the main part of his show. On the stage, the chairs were set out at a three-quarter angle so they faced across the stage as much as they faced the audience. It meant that Will could face us, the audience could see us, but Will was also sort of facing the audience.

'All my volunteers now need to close their eyes and allow themselves to relax. Listen only to my voice and concentrate on it. Let no other thoughts divert your attention from my voice.' His tone was soothing yet commanding at the same time. 'Let yourself relax,' he repeated, asking us to focus on our toes and fingers and let the stress and worry flow out from them. He worked inward to our cores and then had us think of a happy memory. The one which popped unbidden into my head was seeing Jermaine and Barbie at the manor house in Kent for the first time. I had left the ship and thought my friends to be lost to me. I could feel myself smiling but became aware that his technique for making me relax had actually worked.

Maybe there was something to this hokum after all.

Will's voice invaded my dreamy state once more. 'In a moment I will count backwards from three and on the count of one you will open your eyes and find yourself feeling completely relaxed and happy. You will want to meet the person next to you and you will instantly decide that you find them very attractive.'

I heard his words and wondered who might be sitting next to me – I hadn't taken the time to look when I claimed my seat. Then he counted backwards, and my eyes opened. I looked to my right and had to admit I was pleasantly surprised to find a handsome man in his forties looking back at me. He had a natural tan to his skin and bright blue eyes that shone above a pair of full lips. Was this hypnotism working? Did he really look like that or had I sat down next to a less desirable person and the hypnosis altered his image in my head?

Will Controller appeared in front of me and spoke. I swung my head to look up at him.

'Hypnosis does not work on everyone,' he announced to the crowd. 'Some simply cannot achieve the relaxed state that permits my control to invade their thoughts.' Then he dropped his voice to speak only with me, 'I told you earlier, Mrs Fisher. I am not robbing people when they are hypnotised. Please leave my stage now so I may focus on those who are not here to spy on me.'

I pursed my lips and thought about causing a scene, but Will waved to the crowd, begging them to applaud me as I left the stage. Tammy-Jo arrived to guide me away, so I went, muttering inside my head all the way back to my seat with Alistair.

'Patricia?' he repeated my name in the same tone he said it when I went to the stage.

Dropping grumpily into my chair, I said, 'I was curious, that's all.'

The show continued, other persons who Will identified as not being fully hyp-notised were dismissed as well, reducing the number of volunteers to six, which included Mike and Lady Mary. This hadn't been the plan, I just needed them to volunteer and go up there. They could have left at any time once they had shown the power of suggestion was upon them. Watching them now, I could not discern whether they were acting or hypnotised.

Will and Tammy-Jo had the six people paired off. Mike with Lady Mary, then the ringers, Liam and Brenda, and two men which included the potbellied man Tammy-Jo had dragged from the audience. They were supposed to believe they were in a singing contest and auditioning for a part in a show.

Will commanded them, 'When you hear the next piece of music, couple number one will open their eyes and believe that they are Elton John and Kiki Dee singing *Don't go Breaking my Heart.*' He stepped back and cued the music.

Couple number one were the ringers who belted out the lyrics faultlessly though there was no sheet of words to follow. They were convincing too, able to hold a tune better than most would. The music ended and the audience clapped.

'Couple number two, show us what you've got,' Will encouraged them.

'This ought to be good,' I murmured, wondering what couple number two, AKA Mike and Lady Mary might do. Up until now, they hadn't needed to do anything particularly embarrassing, but that was about to change.

The music started, and suddenly Mike had an imaginary microphone in his hand and was singing Elton's lines like he was in a karaoke booth. He was out of tune and off key, but he acted as if none of that mattered. Then Lady Mary sang her line and was equally awful, but just as determined. Together, when they hit the harmony, it was like listening to the sound a donkey might make if a person stuffed a frozen parsnip up its bottom.

Mercifully, the music stopped and couple number three, the two men, got started. In many ways, they were worse, not least because they were both trying to be Elton. The show itself ran for roughly seventy-five minutes, taking us to al-most ten o'clock when Will and Tammy-Jo finished up and left the stage. They went through a routine where they unhypnotized the remaining volunteers and thanked them for participating and advised that the bar would shut in approx-imately thirty minutes. We had deliberately chosen the last show of the day because I was certain the thieves were only striking when they knew it was late and they could be certain of their victims' state.

As planned, Lady Mary and Mike retired to the bar for a drink once they were released from their hypnotic state. I wondered if the last hour might be the longest Lady Mary had gone without a drink while awake since coming on board.

The barmen were darting about, making lots of drinks as many who came in to enjoy the show were gravitating toward the bar for one last beverage before bed. In many ways, I expected that helped them because we all got to watch while barman one talked to Mike and Lady Mary while barman two made their drinks.

Wondering what I am on about? The thing I remembered earlier was how dilated the pupils were on the couple Alistair and I discovered with Zaki and Hamond two nights ago. I thought nothing of it at the time but seeing the two barmen earlier made me question who else, other than Will and Tammy-Jo and the ringer couple were part of the act. The answer was no one, but those involved in the show were not the only people in the bar every night when someone got robbed. The victims all acted confused and couldn't provide details of their attackers not because they were still hypnotised, but because they were drugged.

By the barmen.

In each case, the victims were a couple who had volunteered to be in the hypnotist's show, hence the natural assumption they were confused because they were hypnotised. That wasn't the case though and now it was time to prove it.

Further down the bar, Rick and Akamu ordered drinks, making sure they got the same in their order as Mike and Lady Mary had. Then, moving past them, a quick switcharoo took place and the barmen got to watch their chosen victims drink what they believed to be the drug-laced concoctions. Unseen by them, Alistair tested the drinks using a portable kit. I hadn't seen one before, but Alistair said they were readily available on the internet for a few dollars and they had kits installed in every bar on the ship.

Like a pregnancy test, the little test strip absorbed the liquid and gave a reading. Both drinks flashed red: rohypnol. Was there ever invented a more misused drug? Intended as a sleeping pill, it was a plague upon humanity. Okay we used it ourselves earlier, but ... honestly that's different, okay?

We could have busted the barmen now, but wilfully drugging people wasn't the result we wanted, so we left the bar and the 'victims' behind. I didn't know how much Mike drank in his normal routine, but I got the impression it wasn't much. Lady Mary, in contrast, was probably on her second bottle of gin today. They had to play the part of disorientated, drugged victims, but I believed they wouldn't have to sell it hard. If I were right, and it looked like I was, the barmen would be leaving their posts moments after the last people left the bar, which just happened to be Mike and Lady Mary. It had worked for the barmen at least three times before that we knew of – why wouldn't it work this time?

Our victims wobbled along the passageways arm in arm, watched from a distance by Alistair and the six security guards he posted outside the doors earlier. The rest of us were heading back to the briefing room when my phone rang.

Seeing Alistair's name displayed, I put it on speaker. 'Hi, Alistair.'

'We got them,' he announced. 'They pounced out dressed in capes like Will Controller. I guess that's why the victims were so confused. They are on their way to the brig as we speak. I'll be back with you shortly.'

We ended the call as Rick and the others with me commented on a well-constructed bust. Even Mavis and Agnes, who were generally on the side of the outlaw in such scams, congratulated me. I acknowledged their praise, but it reinforced an idea that formed in my head a few days ago. I hadn't been sure about it until now, but the more thought I gave it, the more it made sense.

All I had to do now was survive the next twenty-four hours. If I could do that, I would broach the subject with Alistair, though I felt sure it was something he would embrace.

Arriving outside the briefing room door, I paused, my heart beginning to thud again because my life hinged on whether the team had managed to crack the code to unlock the mysteries of Verity's journal.

Sad Times

Their faces answered my question long before anyone could speak.

'We're not there yet,' said Barbie, heavily accenting the 'yet' part of her statement for my benefit.

'We still have time,' added Lieutenant Bhukari, but her tone suggested that they were already beginning to question their ability to work it out.

'Have you had any luck at all?' asked Mavis, coming around me and into the room.

The seven people working the computers all glanced between each other – they were getting nowhere. Even Sam's perpetual grin was missing; he understood the gravity of our situation. This was our final roll of the dice. If we couldn't take her down then maybe we could fight, but that meant putting countless lives at stake and I believed her when she said she would find new victims to kill and keep finding them until I gave myself up. She had trillions of dollars at her disposal, plus weapons and people to operate them. Could she get her hands on a submarine and use it to threaten the whole ship?

Probably. The answer swam through my head with much the same effect a diver gets when they see a distinctly shark-shaped shadow go overhead.

I didn't know what I was supposed to do next. Was there a plan B I could devise if I put my mind to it? I had been outmanoeuvred by a wilier adversary than I'd ever faced before. I might have lured the shark to the surface and got it to take my bait, but landing it looked likely to prove a step more than I could manage.

'We're not giving up, madam,' insisted Jermaine. 'Right, chaps?'

His sentiment was echoed by everyone but, honestly, I felt like telling them to call it a day. They had all worked so hard already, all given up so much; how could I ask them for any more?'

When Alistair came through the door behind me a few moments later, I knew what I wanted to do and where I wanted to go. Maybe this wasn't to be my last night on Earth, but I was going to act like it was. I whispered to him, took his hand, and quietly departed the briefing room once more, leaving my friends behind as they continued trying to save my life.

Everything

The hand that clamped over my mouth stifled my scream but only just. Another hand was doing what it could to pin me to the bed so I wouldn't spring from it and start fighting. Alistair, whose arm had been draped across my middle came abruptly awake too. He was going for his gun, which was on the nightstand because we both felt the same sense of fear.

I stopped him, flinging out an arm to arrest his motion because I recognised the blonde locks hanging in front of my face. And as I let the tension ease from my muscles, Barbie removed her hand from my mouth.

'Miss Berkeley, have you news?' Alistair asked as he sat up in my bed. She had to have because she would not have invaded my bedroom otherwise.

'Yes,' she replied, her voice a whisper. 'You'll want to get dressed quickly and quietly. I'll wait for you outside.'

Perplexed, I looked about for the three dachshunds. They stayed in the suite, most likely playing rough and tumble while I was at the cabaret and were petted but soon dismissed when I arrived back at the suite later with Alistair. Their bed was tossed into the suite's main living area because they would try to get on the bed otherwise and that wasn't practical given how we were employing it.

She left without another word, carefully closing the door behind her without making a sound. Alistair and I glanced at each other, but obeyed her request, speedily donning our clothes again. My hair was probably a mess and I had gone to bed with my makeup still on, so that was most likely covering my face to make me look like a half-drowned clown. Both details were insignificant if Barbie had indeed cracked the code and I couldn't stuff my body into my clothes fast enough such was my desperation to find out.

Hurrying out into the main area of my suite, I found Barbie waiting for me by the lobby and Jermaine, in my suite for the first time since he was shot, coming out of Agent Garrett's bedroom. I guess I had been right about the two of them, but I didn't say anything.

Barbie had a finger to her lips, making it clear she wanted to leave the suite before she revealed anything about her discovery. Outside the door were the guards Alistair posted there to protect us while we slept. There were two more guarding the door into Jermaine's adjoining butler's cabin - a trick I learned in my very first week on board. He still didn't know if he could trust them – they might be working for the Godmother – which was why his gun had been ready on the nightstand.

He dismissed them now, sending them to get some sleep because it was 0315 in the morning.

Padding along the passageway, the lack of conversation making our footsteps seem loud, I saw from my window the lights of a city going by on the distant shoreline: Ireland was outside, a place Verity said she wanted to visit. Were we going to spoil her plan?

Unable to take not knowing any longer, I begged Barbie, 'Tell me what you found, please!'

She walked backwards a few paces. 'Everything,' she smiled. Then she pirouetted back the right way and continued walking.

Everything?

'Everything what?' I demanded to know.

Over her shoulder as we rounded the end of the passageway, she said, 'You know how you solve cases in your head and then get the rest of us to do things while you refuse to explain why?'

I puffed out my cheeks. 'I suppose,' I admitted reluctantly, knowing full well I was guilty.

She grinned at me. 'How does it feel to be on the receiving end?'

I was going to throttle her. 'Just tell me what you found, you horrible perfect blonde cow!'

That one made her laugh. Jermaine too and they both smiled at me when they said together. 'Everything.'

My eyes popped out on stalks, but before I could threaten to shove them down the elevator shaft, Barbie started talking.

'We were getting nowhere, right? It had been hours with the seven of us researching cyphers and codes and uploading codebreaking software specifically designed to find patterns in the encrypted sequences. But we got nothing. I think it took us so long to see it because we were all getting tired.'

'See what?' I begged.

'It wasn't a code at all.' I gave her a quizzical look. 'What looked like sequences of letters and numbers with capitals and occasional other symbols such as ampersand or hash was a code, but not one that could be decrypted to form words or sentences.'

Confused, I said, 'I'm not following you. First you said it wasn't a code, then you said it is.'

'That's right,' she replied unhelpfully. 'I couldn't get anywhere so I went back to looking at the footage from Verity's cabin. Watching originally, Jermaine thought she was writing in her journal. When you looked closer, you saw that she was using the journal in conjunction with a computer. When I looked again, I saw that she never changed the page and when she finished what she was doing, she did write in her journal. For three seconds. I timed it. From picking up a pen to putting it down was three seconds. I wrote out the last line of code written in the journal. How long do you think it took me?'

I gave it a wild stab in the dark, 'Three seconds?'

She nodded. 'Yes. The journal isn't full. It looks to be years old, and it probably is, but it is only about three-quarters full. On the last page, the entries only go halfway down.' She was grinning triumphantly when the elevator chimed behind her and we all got in.

I still didn't get it. 'Barbie, you are going to have to spell it out to me.'

'The lines of code are passwords. Randomly generated, daily passwords. Each is sixteen digits long which means to guess them would take a supercomputer a lifetime.'

I screwed up my face. 'Passwords? To what.'

Barbie glanced at Jermaine, who was grinning too. Then she finally said the thing that revealed why they both looked so pleased with themselves. 'Her dark web portal.' My heart stopped for a few seconds. 'You remember a few weeks ago we were at home in the manor house and I found snippets and traces of a character called the Godmother but couldn't access anything because it takes passwords to get inside.' I nodded unable to speak. 'We have the password,' she told me simply. 'I think it is a twenty-four-hour thing. Everyday a new password is generated. We have a tiny window to explore her business transactions and see what we can do with them.'

My heart was pounding in my chest. This was a lottery win. It was the golden ticket to the chocolate factory. Swallowing hard, I asked, 'What did you find so far?'

Jermaine snorted a laugh, glanced at Barbie and together the best friends said, 'Everything!'

The Ladies' Restroom is Full of Surprises

T hey were neither joking nor exaggerating. With access to the Alliance of Families' portal on the dark web, we could see everything. It was run like any other business on the planet with financial statements, quarterly predictions, minutes from meetings. If we kept looking, I would probably find embarrassing pictures from the most recent staff Christmas party. There was a telephone directory, addresses, names, reports ... the list went on. It would take a team of computer forensic people years to delve through all of it, but we had seven people and six computers, and they were doing the best they could.

'I just found a file on drug operations in south east China,' announced Hideki.

'That's nothing,' scoffed Deepa Bhukari. 'I just found thousands of photographs of people the Alliance has killed. The people are dead in the picture at least, and each picture has a file name that provides what I think is the name, date, and location of the person making the hit. The files are arranged by country.'

Lieutenant Schneider piped up next, 'I have a bunch of financial statements from a branch in Chicago and the entries are extortion, guns, human trafficking ... its all here, laid completely bare.'

What they had found was staggering. The question now was what could we do with it?

'We're downloading everything,' Lieutenant Baker told me. 'We had to scare up some multi-terabyte portable hard drives and it still might not be enough, but if the passcode is going to change at some point, we have to get all we can before it does.'

'No indication when it resets?' I asked.

No one knew the answer. 'Most probably at midnight,' said Barbie, 'but we don't know in what time zone.'

I was thinking as fast as I could. 'Okay, so we'll get kicked out at some point, but in the meantime, we are copying everything we can. How long will it take to get it all?' I got a sea of shrugs in response. We had the Godmother in our mitts or, at least, we sort of had her. What we had was enough to convict her and maybe everyone in her organisation. Who could guess how many unsolved crimes we were going to sew up with what we had found? But did it solve the immediate problem?

'There's more,' said Lieutenant Baker. 'We found a file labelled "The Aurelia" which naturally drew our attention. His comment had been aimed at Alistair, who was already moving to see what Baker had to show him. 'There is a list of names, sir,' Baker revealed cautiously, clearly aware that what his captain was about to see was shocking.

Shocking was the right word for it because the Alliance of Families, under Verity's instruction, had researched a number of targets looking for weak spots – persons who they could bribe or coerce into doing their bidding. Some were rejected, but others were shown to have chosen the money offered over loyalty. Maybe they thought they might get away with it. Maybe they believed they wouldn't be called upon to do anything heinous. Whatever the case, they were caught now.

With a steely edge to his voice, Alistair asked, 'Can the downloading and examination of this dark website spare my crew members?' He meant the four lieutenants sat around the table. He wanted them because they were not on the list.

'What are you going to do?' I asked.

Exhaling slowly through his nose, Alistair looked my way and said with a determined growl, 'Fill the brig.'

'You may want this list too then, sir,' said Lieutenant Pippin. 'I think these are all the people in the Godmother's employment who are on the ship posing as passengers. The list contains the three men we already caught, plus the two Agent Garrett shot and it comes with pictures. It looks to be close to a hundred of them.'

A hundred? Verity had brought a hundred assassins on the ship with her. No wonder she had been so calm and confident. Some of the crew she bought, bribed, or blackmailed would have helped her get weapons on board. Who knew what kind of armoury they had at their disposal? But if the menacing look on Alistair's face was anything to go by, they were in trouble now.

Baker and the other three security officers were all getting to their feet and shrugging their shoulders back into their jackets. Alistair closed the distance between us and pulled me into a quick hug. He kissed the side of my face. 'Don't leave this room,' he commanded. 'Promise me, Patricia. We have her now. In the next hour, I will have her people in cuffs and the treacherous members of my crew will be thankful if I haven't tossed them overboard. In a few hours this will be over.'

I let him leave, his officers following him through the door with a sense of purpose combined with a need for justice and the unswervable nervousness that preceded doing anything dangerous. I needed them to all come through this in one piece, but I was feeling a lot more confident of a positive outcome now than I was yesterday evening.

While they were filing through the door, Barbie was signalling to get my attention; there was something else she wanted to show me. She didn't use words, she just pointed to a screen. My jaw dropped open when I saw what she wanted me to see. It made no sense. Literally none at all. Until I thought about it for a minute, and then I could not only see the logic, but understood why.

I patted her arm, and made to move away, but she snagged my arm and held me close so she could whisper to me.

From the far corner of the briefing room, an unexpected snorting noise startled me until a flailing arm appeared from beneath a coat and Sam's face rose into view. Unable to offer much by way of assistance to the code-breaking operation, he'd done the sensible thing and grabbed some shut eye. Something had awoken him, and it turned out to be his phone we saw when he dug around in his pockets and held it up. He spotted me and chucked a wave in my direction; this was all still fun to him.

Having been roused so rudely from my bed, I was yet to visit the restroom and was beginning to feel a distinct need to do so. There wasn't one in the briefing room, so I went to the door.

Jermaine called, 'Madam?' I spun around to see what he wanted. 'May I insist I accompany you if you are planning to leave this room?'

'I need the ladies,' I explained with a frown, not particularly happy at the need to announce my bodily functions.

'I'll go with her,' Barbie volunteered. 'It's just along the passageway on the other side,' she assured him. Then with a sigh because he still wasn't convinced, she added, 'You can watch us from the door.'

'Anyone else want to come?' I enquired snippily. My irritation went unnoticed by Hideki who was too busy with the computers, trying to do the work of about four people now that the security team had gone, and Sam didn't even look up from his phone, frowning at the screen as if he couldn't remember his password.

Barbie opened the door, and to annoy Jermaine, she then peered around the doorframe in an exaggerated secret agent manner. Really needing to go, I went around her and along the passageway where I pushed the door to the ladies open.

Barbie clearly wasn't that desperate to join me because she was joking with Jermaine still in the doorway to the briefing room. They felt like they had cracked this case and were beginning to relax. I wasn't so sure because we still didn't have anyone we could take it to. All the law enforcement agencies were corrupted by the Alliance of Families infiltrating them. So Verity claimed and I believed her.

Then it hit me: amongst all the other information inside the Alliance portal, it was bound to tell us who she had in her employ within the FBI, Interpol, the Swedish secret police and every other law enforcement agency on the planet. If we could expose that ... the possibilities crashed over me like a huge wave but then the door to the restroom swung shut behind me and an arm clamped over my mouth.

Nearly wet myself? Let's just not discuss that subject, eh?

'Please be quiet, Mrs Fisher,' a very British voice insisted. 'I am going to take my hand away. It would be counterproductive if you were to scream.' I wasn't going to scream, but he had been right to clamp his hand over my mouth because I would have if he'd chosen to just announce his presence by speaking.

As his hand came away, I spun around to face him. 'What are you doing here?' I demanded to know, truly wishing he wasn't because I really needed to pee.

What I got in response to my question was a raised eyebrow. 'You sent me a message telling me you were in dire straits and begging I attend if at all possible.'

Still recovering from the shock of his appearance, I tried to clarify my question. 'What I mean is, why are you in the ladies' restroom? Why couldn't you join me in the briefing room like a normal person?'

Now his curious look became one of mystery. 'Because I am not ordinary, Mrs Fisher. To most I do not even exist and my career, indeed often my life, depends on never being seen.'

Okay, I had to give him that. Justin Metcalf-Howe was a British spy and as close to being a true-life James Bond as anyone could hope to get. He was dressed head to toe in black which included a tight-fitting hood that covered all but his face. I first met him when he landed his paraglider on the Aurelia's helipad as we sailed out of Athens. He was being pursued by spies from other nations and convinced me – because I'm sooo stupid – to help him get a data device into the hands of his intended contact in Malta. Well you can guess how that went. Anyway, I figured he owed me so when I started calling in my friends, I sent him a message too.

I never really expected that he would show up though.

'Am I correct to assume you need me to assist you with the Godmother?' he asked, making my jaw drop open.

'How, on Ear ...' The door started to open, cutting off what I was going to say as Barbie came in still chuckling over whatever she and Jermaine had been discussing. As it swung, it blocked both her and my view of Justin the spy who was still standing behind it. Would he leap out on Barbie the same way he had me?

'Everything okay, Patty,' Barbie asked, pausing in the doorway, and holding the door open. 'I thought I heard someone talking.'

Another step brought her into the restroom. I tensed, about to say, 'Look out!' when the door swung shut behind her, but Justin the spy was gone. My eyes bugged from my head as I stared at the space where he had been.

Barbie didn't notice. She was yawning and crossing the restroom to a basin where she splashed some water on her face and declared herself to be bone tired. Questioning if I had seen Justin or imagined him, I went to stand in the space he had occupied and spotted the wall panel that was just slightly ajar.

Wondering how many more shocks my poor heart would have to endure today, I felt thankful that I wouldn't have to see Verity again. She was a truly scary person, most especially since she dropped the façade and showed me her true self last night. In the next hour, Alistair would weed out those members of his crew he now knew were on the Godmother's payroll and he would proceed to take into custody all her assassins dotted about the ship. It was a huge win. I had been worried about whether we would be able to find a law enforcement agency that was clean but armed with the knowledge gleaned from her own dark website, that was no longer so much of a concern.

Yes, there might still be a fight, but I wouldn't have to be a part of it. I thought all this while a sense of absolute relief settled over me.

How wrong I was.

Insurance Policy

I didn't notice the incongruity when I returned to the briefing room. I was feeling excited about the change in our fortunes and the possibility that this was almost all over. The ship had docked in Dublin and once the Godmother was taken into custody along with all her criminal associates, I would be able to go ashore and explore. I might even try a Guinness in a real Irish bar.

I would insist that Alistair take a few hours off to join me, and over lunch or dinner, I would propose to him an idea that now felt less like a dream and more like an opportunity. I was almost giddy with happiness.

When I heard my phone chime an incoming text, I was chatting with Jermaine as he showed me a file of predicted rainfall in Columbia. It was part of a report regarding their cocaine production and yet more damning evidence as if we needed anything else. Crossing to my handbag where it was abandoned on a table near the door, I was thinking about the potential global repercussions of our discovery, and had the phone in my hand for almost a minute while I finished up talking to Jermaine.

When I finally looked down at the screen and opened the message, I stopped breathing and my vision went fuzzy. I had to place a hand on the table to keep myself upright.

The text message contained but a two-word message: *Come alone*. It wasn't the message that threw me, or the fact that Verity sent it. It was the picture.

The lighting was poor, but even so I could see it was the interior of my suite I was looking at. In a line, on their knees, and with guns pointing at their heads, were Melissa and Paul Chalk. Next to them was Agent Garrett, and beside him was Sam. I had believed my young assistant to be asleep under his coat on the chairs in the corner of the briefing room still, but he wasn't. The message he received just before I went to the restroom must have been one to summon him, perhaps a picture of his parents: that would have done it.

To make it just that little bit worse, all three of the dachshunds were on their leads but the man holding them had a cleaver in his other hand. I felt sick and faint and knew I had no choice but to obey.

I had no way of knowing how many troops she had with her. I doubted it was the full compliment she brought onto the ship, but it was enough. Even if Alistair rounded up all the others, he couldn't save the hostages inside my suite.

Feeling disconnected from my body, I placed my phone on the table and glanced over my shoulder: everyone was busy with their computers and no one was looking my way. As quietly as I could, I let myself out and walked away.

Would Verity let them go if I gave myself up? I doubted it, but I also knew I wouldn't be able to live with myself if I denied the Godmother her prize and let them die in my place.

I arrived at the door to my suite a few minutes later unaware about how I got there. My feet obeyed the command to go from A to B but at no point was my brain connected enough to notice the journey. Standing in the passageway outside, I realised my doorcard was in my handbag which I'd left in the briefing room. My phone was there too, so I couldn't even send Alistair a final goodbye message. I cursed myself, but did it really matter?

The sun was hours away from rising yet. The panoramic windows behind me showed a dark Dublin skyline barely discernible from the sky itself. Raising a trembling right hand, I knocked on my own door.

The sound of my knuckles in the silent passageway seemed startlingly loud, but the door was ripped open by a brutish man with a machine gun who wasted no time with introductions as he grabbed my hair and yanked me across the threshold.

A cry of pain escaped my lips but he released me the next second, taking his free hand from my hair to then shove me off balance and into the main living area where I fell to the carpet feeling wretched and alone.

The four hostages were still on their knees. They were facing me as if arranged so they would be the first thing I saw on my arrival. Melissa and Paul were both shaking with fear and Paul had a busted lip and black eye.

Curled on my favourite couch with a cup of tea was Verity. She was leafing through a magazine.

'You said it would just be me,' I blurted.

My outburst forced her to look up for the first time since I came into the room. Closing the magazine and putting it to one side, she said, 'And I thought your assistant to be dead. Imagine my surprise when my people stopped Mr and Mrs Chalk and discovered they had messages from Sam that arrived after I had him shot. I was grabbing them anyway ... a little insurance policy just in case you tried anything silly today, but your treachery annoyed me, Patricia.' She turned her head to look at her husband, Walter, standing just behind and to the side of her. 'That's what I said, isn't it, Walter? That I was annoyed.'

Walter croaked out a one-word reply, 'S'right.'

'Well, I don't like being annoyed, Patricia. So I'm afraid there has to be a forfeit.' I was terrified beyond the capacity for rational thought, but I did my best and looked about the room. There were eight men, plus Walter and Verity making it ten in total. Four stood behind the hostages, each with a handgun pointed squarely at the head of the person kneeling in front. With Verity and Walter by the couch, that left three men. One was behind me somewhere, out of sight but over toward the door and the other two were by the kitchen. I took all that in, but I had no plan for the information.

Seeing the thing that was missing, I asked. 'Where are the dogs?'

Verity snorted her disgust. 'Always with the dogs, Patricia. It is so tiresome. They are in the oven. I'll turn it on when we leave. I wanted to do it already, but the horrible little rats would probably just make annoying noises while they cooked.'

Bile rose in my throat as I wondered how anyone could ever be so cruel. Biting down my fear, I looked up at her face from my position on the carpet. 'I took your journal last night while we were having dinner,' I told her. I didn't know what I was doing, but I had to try something.

Her face registered surprise, but then disbelief when she reached down to her handbag on the carpet and picked the journal out to show me. 'You mean this one?' she scoffed.

'Yes,' I licked my lips nervously. 'I have a team of friends on board including a detective from England. We were on to you from the start. Last night we swiped the journal, copied its contents, and put it back in your bag without you noticing it. You were not the only one with people inside the restaurant.'

Her amused smile faded, changing to a scowl as she considered my words. The journal was stuffed angrily back into her handbag. 'And? So what, Patricia? Do you think you can use the contents against me? Is that your plan? I'm afraid that won't work.'

'Why not?' I asked, buying just a little more time. Time for what, I didn't know, but continuing to live felt like the right thing to do.

Verity chuckled at my question. 'You see, Patricia? This is why you could never beat me. I looked you up, you know. When you survived the second assassination attempt, I got curious. You attended an ordinary comprehensive school and achieved mediocre grades. Your employment record is dismal and a demonstration that you never once tried to stretch yourself. Did the word ambition ever enter your mind? The journal contains a code to access a highly sophisticated data management system,' She glanced at her watch, 'and the most recent code just changed so even if you are telling me the truth, which I do not believe you are, the information in the journal is now of no use.'

I nodded. 'That's right, Verity, but we accessed your dark web portal hours ago.' Her smile froze – how could I know about the dark web portal? 'Everything you have ever done, the identity of all the members of the Alliance of Families, their holdings, their crimes … everything,' I used the word Barbie and Jermaine employed to describe what they found. 'Not only is it all there, but we have been able to copy it.'

Her eyes narrowed as she considered what I had just told her. The men in the room were all looking her way uncertainly; if I was telling the truth, their identities were no longer secret. Then Verity blew out a breath as if staggered by my revelation. 'I have to hand it to you, Patricia. I am impressed, and that doesn't happen very often. This will cause me a severe headache and no mistake. I will have to bribe or blackmail dozens of people to make sure none of the information you have obtained is ever seen. Honestly, I probably won't get anything else done this morning.' She leaned forward, peering around the hostages to a man near the kitchen. 'Horace?'

Horace hadn't been paying much attention and almost jumped when she called his name. 'Yes, ma'am?'

'Wake Teddy, will you please? I'll need him to make some adjustments to the portal. I want new security in place and the whole thing shifted to a new location. He needs to get on it right away. Also, get the crew we bought from the ship's security detail; I want them here now. They need to find Patricia's people and retrieve everything they have. I want bodies in bags within the hour.'

Horace already had his phone out. 'Yes, ma'am.'

'Better yet,' Verity added. 'Get them all up. I think it's time I got a little medieval with the people on this ship. Perhaps killing one in ten of the passengers and crew will do it. What do you think, Patricia? This is because of you after all. I've always been fond of the word decimate – to reduce by one tenth. It was an old Roman punishment I believe. The displeased centurion would have every tenth man slaughtered. You can watch, Patricia. Then I'll kill you.'

While the world felt like it was spinning out of control beneath my feet, and I wondered, yet again, if I might just throw up, Horace had the phone to his ear.

'I don't hear you talking to anyone, Horace,' snapped Verity impatiently. 'Why are you not passing on my messages?'

'Um, no one is answering, ma'am,' Horace gulped, fiddling with his phone, and putting it to his ear again.

Wondering if I still had the power of speech, I managed to croak, 'We found the file that identified the ship's crew in your employment. Alistair started rounding them up a while ago. So too the list of your hired assassins on the ship. Maybe Horace should call the brig,' I suggested.

Everyone in the room was facing me which meant I was the only one looking in the direction that showed me the windows. A few seconds ago, I spotted something. It was black outside, but the light from inside the suite illuminated what looked like a rope when it appeared from above. My level of terror hadn't dropped, but when a second rope appeared, and then a third, I made sure I was looking at Verity and not the windows.

Verity, otherwise known to the world as the Godmother was glaring at me. I had taken her through the annoyed stage and out the other side. She was going to do something terrible in the next second and all I could do was pray she did it to me and not one of the hostages.

Her mouth began to open as she swung her head to look at the man holding a gun to Sam's head. And that was when it happened.

The Internet is a Wondrous Thing

Remember the flashbang? Yeah, that thing is a child's toy. In the space between Verity opening her mouth and the first word forming, I got to meet the adult version.

The windows of the suite, all the way along the wall in the main living area exploded inwards as one. A flash so bright it felt as if it lasered my brain into two pieces, lit the room to the accompaniment of the sort of noise a volcano makes when it explodes. I was hurled over backwards by the strength of the blast but before I hit the carpet, shots were being fired.

My brain registered that I was hearing controlled bursts fired in a confident manner and that no shots were being wasted. The shots all sounded the same too as if Verity's people hadn't managed to return fire at all.

I bounced once and came to rest and by then it was over. A face appeared above me, a hand inside a black glove reaching down to help me from the deck. When I saw the first rope, I assumed it was a rescue attempt and that Justin the British super spy was about to crash through the window. When more ropes appeared, it confused me, but as he hauled me to my feet, I discovered my first guess was on the money. It was Justin, and he had a squad of friends along for the fun.

186

A dozen men, looking like the SAS and armed to the teeth with an arsenal of lethal weaponry had shot all of Verity's men in less time than it took me to fall to the deck. Verity was still sitting on the couch but now her eyes were as wide as saucers.

Melissa and Paul were hugging each other and crying again, terrified beyond belief, but remembering Sam, they both threw themselves at him and the reunited family hugged and cried in the middle of my suite.

Wayne got unsteadily to his feet, looking shocked to still be alive.

A noise from just behind Verity drew my attention and I looked across the room to find Walter staring down at his chest. He pulled open his jacket to reveal a growing bloodstain on his white shirt. Looking back up again, he stared at the ceiling and closed his eyes. 'Oh, thank goodness,' he whispered just loud enough for us to hear. 'I couldn't take another day married to that cow.'

His statement shocked Verity, but before she could respond, he crashed to the deck, dead as a nail.

Justin said, 'I believe the crew will probably be alerted by the noise, Mrs Fisher. You seem to be in safe hands once again so the chaps and I will leave you with your bodyguard and make good our escape.' He didn't hang around to gauge my opinion, he simply started running.

For what felt like the tenth time since I awoke, my jaw dropped open as his whole team ran back to the destroyed windows and dove through them, vanishing over the side of the ship as if they had never been here.

Justin was right in that people would start appearing any moment now, but they were not here yet, and if Verity's expression were anything to go by, she still didn't think she was beaten.

'Think you've won, do you, Patricia?' she goaded. 'Agent Garrett, kill her.'

Agent Garrett pulled his gun from his shoulder holster proving that he'd never been disarmed and was being used as a dummy hostage the whole time.

I backed away a pace. 'But you protected me,' I blurted. 'You dived in front of a bullet for me.'

'On my instruction, Patricia,' bragged Verity. 'You were to die when I was ready and not before. Agent Garrett knew that and knew what would happen to him if you were killed before I gave the order. He had to kill those two idiots yesterday too. We'll never know why they panicked and went for their weapons. It was probably confusion because they recognised Agent Garrett, but he was right to make sure they were silenced. '

'That's why you shot Schooner, isn't it?' I asked her, seeing the truth of it for myself.

Agent Garrett had his gun pointing at me, but he was waiting for the Godmother to give him the nod.

She grinned at me. 'I couldn't let that maniac finish you. That wouldn't have been anywhere near good enough. This will do though.' She nodded at Agent Garrett. 'Kill her.'

My heart beat really fast as I watched the muscles in his hand tighten. The trigger clicked and the hammer fell but no bullet exploded from the barrel. Confused, he stared at the weapon, then aimed it and pulled the trigger again.

Still nothing.

'You might be missing something vital,' announced Jermaine as he entered the suite via the butler's adjoining cabin. His sling was gone which might have fooled Agent Garrett if he didn't know it was only a few days since Jermaine got shot. My butler held something in his hand. I couldn't see it, but I knew what it was already because Barbie let me know what Jermaine had been doing when I spotted him leaving Agent Garrett's room earlier.

'My firing pin,' growled Agent Garrett.

Jermaine's stride didn't break as he continued to advance across the room, talking as he came. 'I took the liberty of removing it a few hours ago when we discovered your name among a list of law enforcement persons employed by Mrs Tuppence.' I knew this too because Barbie showed me the information on her computer.

Wayne turned toward him, throwing the gun with intent to harm, and following it up as he charged. Some time ago, he'd boasted that he was better than Jermaine. We were about to find out and my terror returned with a vengeance.

Jermaine ducked the gun, which flew over his head to smash against the far wall in the kitchen. Agent Garrett leapt into the air and was scything down with a clubbing fist as Jermaine came back up. Beyond him, I saw Barbie coming into the suite through the butler's entrance, but my focus was on the fight now taking place.

Jermaine twisted away, catching only a glancing blow from Agent Garrett's fist, which was quickly followed through with a high elbow. The elbow was parried away, my butler never taking his eyes from his opponent as he danced backward to gain space. Reversing direction suddenly just as Agent Garrett lunged after him, he landed a cruel blow to the treacherous policeman's chest.

It stunned Agent Garrett, but only momentarily as he blocked the next strike and kicked out with a leg. The kick would have landed had Jermaine not reacted with his usual lightning speed. Almost defying the laws of physics, his own leg was there to halt the kick, and then flick upward.

Having checked Wayne's latest attack, he was sufficiently off balance for Jermaine's kick to land. The thud as his foot connected with Agent Garrett's ribs made me wince even though I ought to be cheering, but the next strike hit Jermaine's wounded shoulder, drawing a gasp from the tall Jamaican. It showed how weak he was and as he moved back to get out of range, Agent Garrett moved in to press home his advantage.

From the corner of my eye, I spotted Verity moving. She was going for one of the guns dropped by her men. I'd been caught napping, too busy watching Jermaine and Agent Garrett to consider the danger still present and unaccounted for. She was too far away for me to get to before she got her hands on the gun, but that's because I'm a lot slower in my fifties than I was thirty years ago. Even at that age, I was still a snail compared to Barbie who was running across the room to intercept the Godmother before she could turn the tide once again.

She had a laptop in her hands, which I thought she might throw as a weapon. However, she perhaps thought it too precious, or trusted her speed to do what was needed because she used a chair as a springboard, deposited the laptop on a table as she pirouetted through the air in a somersault and landed with her feet either side of the gun Verity was about to pick up.

With a triumphant, 'I don't think so, babe,' she kicked the gun away and shoved Verity back onto the couch.

I didn't know which fight to watch, and I thought it spoke volumes about my battered emotional and mental state that it hadn't once occurred to me to pick up one of the dropped weapons. I could shoot Agent Garrett, or I could threaten to, at least. But just as it occurred to me to end this awful business, I saw Wayne reel backward. Jermaine's right foot was spinning back to the carpet after connecting with his opponent's chin, but as Wayne attempted to recover, Jermaine snagged his left arm, twisting it with the momentum of his own body. Agent Garrett lifted off the carpet, out of control as Jermaine swung him around.

There was a fraction of a second when Wayne was hanging motionless in the air, then Jermaine drove him down into the deck. He slammed down hard, air bursting from his lungs. The fight in Agent Garrett left him and though he was still conscious, he was beaten, and he knew it.

The door to my suite slammed open, my heart banging with shock but not surprise as I knew ship security would be coming: Justin's explosion would have been heard all over the ship.

Jermaine was okay. Barbie was okay. The Chalks were rattled to their core but would survive. And now my suite was filling with faces I knew, and best yet knew I could trust, as Lieutenant Baker led a swarm of white uniforms through my door.

My head swung across to the other side of my suite as yet more poured through the butler's door, these ones led by Lieutenant Schneider. Alistair was on his shoulder and every one of them was toting an assault rifle, issued from the armoury in haste, no doubt. They swept through the kitchen and across the suite cuffing Agent Garrett when Jermaine stepped away from him.

It was done. It was over. Incredible, despite everything, we have won.

Verity's chuckle grabbed everyone's attention.

She was sitting on the couch still, the magazine back in her lap as she nonchalantly flicked through its pages. 'I will say you proved to be a worthy adversary after all, Patricia,' she granted me as if her praise were a thing I might care about. 'The damage you have done will take some time to fix, and doubtless I am about to be arrested, but that won't matter because I will be out by tomorrow. You see, I have enough politicians and figures of influence who got where they are because of me that no charges will ever be brought. I will not stand trial and I will not go to jail. Your interference is little more than an inconvenience.'

I was trying to think of something cutting to say, but Barbie beat me to it. 'I rather think you are in a good deal more trouble than you expect,' she said as she went back to the laptop she brought with her.

Verity smiled at her. 'What is it you think you are going to show me. Evidence? Whatever information you managed to download will not matter. I own the police. I own the police everywhere.'

Barbie didn't pay her any attention as she opened the laptop, clicked the mouse, and typed something. Then she turned the screen around to show a photograph of Verity on the screen. 'You're going viral,' she announced with a grin. 'You're getting more hits than Beyonce's new music video.'

I had no idea what she was talking about and neither did Verity who started to get off the couch. The sound of about thirty assault rifles being cocked convinced her to stay put, but with a cheerful smile, Barbie said, 'I'll come to you.'

'One moment, please, Miss Berkeley,' begged Alistair. Lieutenant Baker moved in with a set of cuffs, taking great pleasure in slapping them into place on Verity's wrists. He then hauled her from the couch to pat her down for hidden weapons. Declaring her safe, Alistair nodded Barbie forward but we all went, far too curious to hang back. What was it Barbie was trying to show Verity?

She started to explain as she set the laptop down where most people could see it. 'I remembered something Patty said about the Godmother being untouchable because she uses terror tactics and money to buy protection from prosecution and that we would never know who to share the information with.'

'That's right, Blondie,' Verity smirked.

'So we posted it online,' Barbie concluded.

Verity tilted her head to one side. 'You did what?'

'We posted it,' Barbie repeated. 'All your transactions and records. The files on politicians your Alliance has corrupted. The pictures of murders. Lists of the members of your organisations, the corrupt law enforcement agents, your bank accounts. Things like the drugs operations, the buyers, couriers, pushers, and everything else complete with home addresses and phone numbers. It's all on the internet. We pushed your videos to YouTube. We gave the world every piece of hidden information because how can they fail to act now? The President of the United States will be able to see exactly who is controlling illegal weapons move-ment, the drug trade, and all the other organised crime operations in America. Do you think you stand a chance? Because it won't be just him and America that will come for you. Every government in every country has the opportunity for a big political win and every law enforcement agency on the planet now knows who their corrupt members are. All over the world, the people you have working for you just got burned. It's over. You're done.' As Barbie's words faded away, Verity saw the truth of it. Whatever else we might have tried in a bid to beat her and get a conviction to stand, none of it could have come close to this. Every crime for however many decades they had been in operation was now exposed and there would be nowhere to hide.

'You did it to yourself,' I sniggered remembering something she bragged about last night. 'You united everyone, brought them up to date and consolidated them into one system. Because of that, we were able to see everything. Your arrogance allowed us to access it all with just one code. A code you wrote in a book.' I was laughing in her face. It wasn't like me, but I couldn't help myself, and now I had started, others were laughing too. Barbie joining in, then Alistair, and soon it seemed like the world was laughing at her.

'I'll kill you,' she growled through gritted teeth. 'I'll kill you all.'

'No,' I replied, my mirth running its course. 'You'll go to jail and never see the light of day again.'

Life Changes

There was a lot of follow up work after Verity was taken away. She cursed and spat and howled profanities until she was out of range, but her words had no impact on me because I didn't believe them. She was powerless now.

The first thing I did, was open the oven to rescue the dogs. Three curious, yet happy dachshund faces peered out at me. Had they been terrified by the experience? No, not one bit. To get them in, Verity's people had taken out a shelf, but the three dachshunds then had room to move about and had busied themselves licking the tiny, burnt bits of food from the deepest crevices of the oven. They had crispy, dirty whiskers and jowls and happy expressions. I think, had I simply closed the oven door again, they would have been completely happy.

Despite that assessment, I took them out and after some fussing, I tucked them away in my bedroom with a chewy treat each. There they would be out of the way and not underfoot because my suite was full of people. Quite a few of them were dead.

My suite wasn't exactly destroyed, but it certainly wasn't liveable either. I had to explain to everyone about Justin Metcalf-Howe and his colleagues because there were nine dead bodies on the carpet and bullet holes everywhere. It wasn't the first time. The rest of the Godmother's people had been rounded up and would be taken off the ship once the main bulk of passengers had been allowed to disembark in a few hours.

I had Jermaine back, that was one of the best parts of winning, but while the dust continued to settle and the security team started to deal with the dead bodies, I led Barbie into the kitchen area because there were other items of administration to deal with.

It was cold in the suite with most of the exterior wall missing, no doubt about it. Seeing me shiver, Jermaine asked, 'Shall I fetch a coat for you, madam?' He had his left arm back in the sling in deference to the injury sustained when he got shot. Fighting with Agent Garrett had no doubt set his recovery back but though I wanted to make him take a seat and relax, I knew he would be happier getting on with things.

'Thank you, Jermaine,' I replied. 'That would be lovely.'

'And perhaps some tea, madam?' he asked, his right hand hovering by the kettle.

A warm smile spread across my face. Something had changed in the last few minutes and I knew what it was: happiness was returning. 'Tea would be delightful.'

My butler filled the kettle and went to fetch a coat from my bedroom, threading his way through the people getting busy in my suite under Alistair's direction. I brought my attention back to my blonde friend.

'Where is Hideki,' I asked her.

'He stayed in the briefing room, uploading the data. I found your phone and saw the picture, but all I told him was that Jermaine and I needed to do something. He has no idea that all this happened or that it is all over. I really ought to tell him, I guess,' she reached for her phone.

'Get him to come here,' I suggested.

Putting the phone to her ear while she waited for her call to connect, she said, 'Good idea.'

Jermaine returned, and shortly there was tea.

Warming her hands on her mug, Barbie asked, 'What happens now? We're going back to East Malling, right?'

Jermaine paused to listen to my answer. I believed he would go wherever I led, but I wanted to factor his needs and hopes into my decision. I didn't want to give up my home in Kent, but I also wasn't prepared to allow my relationship with Alistair to end and that had created an unexpected need to balance many things. Barbie wanted to return to East Malling so she could be with Hideki, but her relationship with him had been strained for weeks because he was a junior doctor at a busy London hospital and worked far too many hours.

I didn't want to answer her question yet, and thankfully I didn't have to because Hideki chose that moment to arrive. He came through the suite's main door looking around with surprised eyes. He had to step to one side when a stretcher went by with a body loaded on it.

Coming over to us with a puzzled expression, he said, 'When you said there had been a fight, but the Godmother was in custody, I didn't realise you meant a gun battle. It looks like a warzone in here.'

Barbie drew him into a hug. 'Sorry, babes. I should have made it clearer.'

Jermaine held a mug in the air as a question, then poured Hideki a cup of tea when he nodded. When the Japanese doctor settled onto a barstool, I caught his attention and nodded: it was time.

Hideki took hold of Barbie's hand and made sure she was looking at him.

'What is it, babe?' she asked, a touch of concern creeping into her voice.

'Would you like to stay on the ship?' he asked.

Her answer was immediate. 'No, Hideki, I want to be with you. I'm coming back to England.'

He bit his lip and asked, 'What if you could do both?' she raised her eyebrows, puzzled by his question. He tried to clarify for her. 'What if you could stay on the ship and see me?' he asked.

'I don't get it,' she replied. 'You're a junior doctor at a London hospital.'

'But I can be a junior doctor anywhere,' he countered. 'There is an open position on this ship.'

Her hands flew to her mouth and tears formed in the corners of her eyes as they began to well up. Dr Kim's death was a terrible tragedy, but he had to be replaced, and though by right the replacement was supposed to be a fully certified doctor with at least some surgical training, and not a junior fresh from school, Alistair had swung it for Hideki to complete his training on board with Dr Davis.

Overwhelmed by what this meant, Barbie threw herself at her boyfriend, wrapping him into a bearhug. But then she broke it suddenly when another thought occurred to her and there were yet more tears in her eyes when she looked at Jermaine and me.

'I'm so happy,' she cried. 'But I'm also so sad because I'll miss you both too much.'

I laughed at her and said, 'I'm staying too.'

She gasped and shoved off from Hideki to throw herself at me instead, and then at Jermaine, squeezing us as if she were trying to crush the life from our bodies.

'Oh, my goodness, I'm so happy,' she cried, tears rolling down her cheeks.

A shout from over by the door heralded yet more arrivals as Rick and Akamu shoved their way into the ruin of my suite.

'We heard an explosion,' said Akamu. 'I bet Rick fifty bucks it was you.'

'I didn't take that bet,' said Rick.

Behind him were the Irish ladies, Mavis and Agnes, and shortly thereafter Lady Mary and Detective Sergeant Mike Atwell. They took a look around my suite at the missing windows and bullet holes and the unwelcome stains on the carpet.

Being unkind, Rick said, 'Now it looks more like a place I would associate with you, Patricia. This is exactly how I would expect your house to be decorated. They ought to patch up the windows and leave the rest until you move out. You know, just to save themselves from having to do it all again in a week's time.'

I shot him a mean look, but said, 'I can't stay in here even if I am staying on the ship. I simply cannot afford it and the cruise line has been more than generous with me already. I believe I will be moving into the captain's quarters.' Once I'd said it, I glanced up at Jermaine and put my hand on his.

We both knew what this meant. He was the butler in the Windsor suite and would soon have new principles staying here that he needed to serve. We would still see each other and perhaps get together when he had time off, but our relationship would be changed, and I could see no way to prevent that.

Barbie asked, 'What will you do about your detective business back home?'

It was a good question, but I had one idea. Swinging my head around to focus on one face, I asked, 'How about it, Mike?'

Jolted by suddenly having everyone look his way, Mike jerked a thumb at himself. 'Me? You want me to take over your business?'

'Take care of it, perhaps,' I suggested. 'Your retirement is coming up anyway, this could be a second career. You've often said how the politics of being in the police bored you and that the only bit you truly enjoyed was solving the mysteries. This is your chance to do it for yourself. I even have an assistant for you.' I was going to have to break the news to Sam that I wasn't coming back full time. I had some things to iron out with Alistair, of course, but felt confident he and I would spend his holidays and annual time off in Kent, and perhaps I would go home sometimes by myself: I was not entirely sold on a life perpetually travelling the planet.

Mike scratched his head. 'I'll need to give that some thought, Patricia,' he said, but he gave me a grin and I was fairly sure he was going to take the offer.

Jermaine handed out more tea for the new arrivals, and they fell into talking about the latest development with the Godmother, Barbie explaining about the dark web and finding my phone and how Agent Garrett was a bad guy all along. I drifted away, leaving them to it. After freeing them from the oven, the three dachshunds had been locked in my bedroom for the last half an hour because they kept barking at the security officers going back and forth. I was also worried they would worry the bodies if they got a chance. Collecting them, I went to find Alistair.

He was outside in the passageway. The panoramic windows now looked out over Dublin which was coming to light as the first tendrils of dawn finally started to scare away the gloom. When I found him, he was just handing over to Commander Philips, who looked startled to see me again.

He gave me a curt nod, 'Mrs Fisher.'

I returned his nod but with a smile added. 'Commander Philips. So sorry for the subterfuge the other day.'

'I understand that it was necessary, Mrs Fisher. Nothing further need be said.'

Alistair left the Commander to his duties, coming to me with a twinkle in his eye. 'What's next for Patricia Fisher then?' he asked.

It was a leading question, but one I welcomed. 'Actually, there is something I need to discuss with you.'

He hitched his right eyebrow. 'Oh, really?'

I slipped my arm through his and began walking, the three little dogs pulling us along. 'You asked me once to join you here and stay with you in your quarters.' Alistair didn't say anything, choosing instead to stay quiet and let me say whatever it was I wanted to say. 'If that offer is still open, I think I would like to take you up on it.'

He drew in a deep and satisfied-sounding breath through his nose. 'Nothing could make me happier, Patricia.'

I patted his arm with my hand. 'Then I will need a few stewards to move my things later today if you think you can spare them. My suite is in need of some repairs anyway.'

'It will be done,' he assured me.

'I'm not done yet.' He looked down at me. 'I cannot just be the captain's woman,' I told him, and as he opened his mouth to say something, I cut him off quickly. 'I'm not talking about changing that to be your wife either. I'm still married for that matter, which is another thing I need to deal with soon. What I mean is, I need a job to keep me busy if I am to stay on board the ship with you.'

'A job?' his forehead was creased in confusion, probably wondering what on Earth I was proposing to do.

'Your security team are very good, but they are just that: a security team. This ship needs a detective.'

Alistair pursed his lips. 'And that would be you?'

I stopped walking and turned inward so I was facing him. 'Do you think you can swing that with Purple Star? That's my caveat, Alistair. I need purpose. I'll stay. I want to stay,' I added in case that wasn't clear. 'But I have to carry on being my own person.' Sensing that he was about to say yes, I blurted, 'And I want to keep Sam as my assistant, but he gets a uniform.' It hadn't even crossed my mind to keep Sam with me until that very moment. I hadn't spoken to him and couldn't imagine what Melissa and Paul might say, but if he wanted to stay with me, that was what I wanted too.

Alistair frowned. 'I don't know, Patricia. That last bit might be a tough sell.'

'Why?' I demanded. 'Because he has Downs?'

Alistair frowned at me. 'You know that's not something I care about.'

'Then you'll have to make Purple Star not care either, darling.' I added the word 'darling' deliberately, then said, 'Please,' in a pleading tone.

'Ship's detective, eh? The things a man must do for love. I guess I'd better go and make a few phone calls.' He kissed me, then let go of my arm and backed away a pace. 'I'll catch up with you soon, Patricia, I want to show you Dublin.'

I smiled, feeling like my heart was full. Not just because of Alistair, but because of everything. The threat which had been hanging over my head for months was finally gone. Barbie and Hideki were together, I was going to get to see Dublin with a whole gang of my good friends, and there was so much to look forward to.

I waved Alistair goodbye and turned away to let the dogs have a proper walk. Do you know what happened next? That cheeky git smacked me on the bum again.

The End

Book 9 is waiting for you. Scan the QR code with your phone to find your copy of Murder is an Artform.

What's next for Patricia Fisher?

When a famous artist comes on board with his wife, his manager, who just happens to be his ex-wife, his ex-wife's lover and his three muses, it's no surprise when someone ends up dead.

They are sailing from Dublin to Southampton, not exactly a long leg, but a lot can happen in a few hours on a cruise ship.

Author's Notes

H ello,

Thank you for reading this book. I hope you enjoyed it and I wonder if you are one of those who found this book by chance. Did you read it and wonder what might have come before? Or did you find me and Patricia long ago and follow her journey from the first page of the first book? I would love everyone to start the journey at book one, but I have no control over such things and must assume people join the story at many different points.

I found Stephanie Plum by Janet Evanovich in the English section of a German airport many years ago and joined that series at book seven. It didn't spoil the effect, but it did send me scurrying to find the start of the series so I could get the most from it.

This story was the culmination of almost a year's work, but it is just a stopping off point because Patricia isn't done yet. Not by a long way. As the ending indicates, she is about to enter a new chapter in her life. She will be on the ship and off the ship as the books continue, for she still needs to return home and finalise that darned divorce.

In this book I used the word entrée, but I chose to employ it in the American usage where it describes the main course of a three-course meal. In Europe, the entrée is the first course, and British people (among others) reading this book might have tutted at my misuse of the term.

To give this book a time marker for those reading it many years from now, it is right before Hallowe'en in 2020 and the UK, and indeed most of the world, is in Covid meltdown. We look set to be forced into another national lockdown any day now and many European countries have already taken that step this week.

My five-year-old's biggest concern is that Santa isn't in our bubble and thus will not be allowed into our house to deliver presents this Christmas. I explained that he is magical and therefore Covid cannot affect him.

It's late here, as it so often is when I finish my books. I tend, once I am near the end, to just go until they are done, unable to sleep until the battle is over and good guys have found a way to triumph. I have a rum and coke to sip as a celebration of another chapter in Patricia's life completed, but soon I will fire this one off into the editing pile and start to consider the next book. My life is a perpetual cycle of book idea after book idea and my house is filled with A4 pads of hastily scribbled notes, which often not even I can decipher.

Not that I am complaining, I love what I do and it means I get to walk my son to school each day and then be there to collect him when he finishes. How many jobs allow that kind of flexibility?

I'm going to leave it there, I really do need to get some sleep.

Take care

Steve Higgs

Free Books and More

Want to see what else I have written? Go to my website.

https://stevehiggsbooks.com/

Or sign up to my newsletter where you will get sneak peeks, exclusive giveaways, behind the scenes content, and more. Plus, you'll be notified of Fan Pricing events when they occur and get exclusive offers from other authors because all UF writers are automatically friends.

Copy the link carefully into your web browser.

https://stevehiggsbooks.com/newsletter/

Prefer social media? Join my thriving Facebook community.

Want to join the inner circle where you can keep up to date with everything? This is a free group on Facebook where you can hang out with likeminded individuals and enjoy discussing my books. There is cake too (but only if you bring it).

https://www.facebook.com/groups/1151907108277718

Made in the USA
Coppell, TX
05 May 2025

49022224R00125